Excel

ADVANCED SKILLS

ENGLISH

YEAR 2

AGES 7–8

READING AND COMPREHENSION WORKBOOK

Get the Results You Want!

PASCAL PRESS

Donna Gibbs &
Tanya Dalgleish

Reprinted 2016, 2017, 2019, 2020, 2021

Updated in 2023 for the NSW Curriculum and Australian Curriculum Version 9.0 changes

Reprinted 2025

ISBN 978 1 74125 569 0

Pascal Press
PO Box 250
Glebe NSW 2037
www.pascalpress.com.au

Publisher: Vivienne Joannou
Project editor: Mark Dixon
Edited by Michael Wyatt
Proofread by Mark Dixon
Answers checked by Glenda Walsh
Cover and page design by DiZign Pty Ltd
Typeset by Kim Webber
Printed by Vivar Printing/Green Giant Press

CONTENTS

How to use this book **2**

Reading strategies **4**

1. Skimming 4
2. Visualising 4
3. Connecting 4
4. Predicting 4
5. Inferring 5
6. Monitoring 5
7. Judging 5
8. Scanning 5

Step-by-step guide to reading texts **6**

SECTION 1

Types of questions **8**

Step-by-step guide to fact-finding questions 8

Fact-finding questions 10

Step-by-step guide to synthesis questions 18

Synthesis questions 20

Step-by-step guide to inferring questions 28

Inferring questions 30

Step-by-step guide to language questions 38

Language questions 40

Step-by-step guide to judgement questions 48

Judgement questions 50

SECTION 2

Bringing it all together **58**

Mixed questions 58

SECTION 3

Answers **82**

Marking grid **106**

How to use this book

This book is designed to help students improve their reading comprehension skills and become more competent, reflective and critical readers.

It provides a step-by-step method of answering different types of comprehension questions, including those in standardised tests such as NAPLAN. Students are taught the strategies to read effectively.

It caters for students with different reading ages by sequencing the texts from easy to more difficult within each chapter and section; and by ordering the type of question dealt with from easy to more difficult.

The book is organised in three sections. Before you begin working through these sections notice the eight useful strategies to use when reading on pages 4–5, and the Step-by-step guide on pages 6–7 that tells you how to answer different types of questions.

Section 1 Types of questions

This section deals with the five question types covered in the book. There is a chapter on each type: fact-finding, inferring, synthesis, language and judgement.

Each chapter begins with a sample reading text and Step-by-step guide to reading that text and answering the particular comprehension questions. This is the teaching opportunity for the question type. Subsequent texts in each chapter provide practice opportunities.

Included on each page is a *Now write!* activity. These writing practice activities support students' reading development and understanding of the types of texts in this book. Students will require additional paper to complete the tasks. Also included at the bottom of each page is a *Note* for the parent or teacher, which summarises additional teaching points relevant to the text on the page.

There are six questions for each text. These are mostly multiple choice but at least one question per text requires a short written answer.

Section 2 Bringing it all together

Mixed questions

This section provides 24 reading texts with mixed question types for further practice and assessment of students' understanding.

The texts are sequenced in order of reading difficulty beginning with the easiest. The questions for each text are also sequenced in order of difficulty beginning with fact-finding questions. Judgement questions require higher-order thinking skills so are dealt with last.

The following set format applies to the 24 texts in the mixed questions section.

- Questions 1 and 2 are fact-finding questions.
- Question 3 is a synthesis question.
- Question 4 is an inferring question.
- Question 5 is a language question.
- Question 6 is a judgement question.

This consistent format provides a scaffold for younger students as they become familiar with the different types of questions and the terminology.

SECTION 3 Answers

This section explains why answers are correct or incorrect. A suitable written answer is supplied for each short-answer question. The multiple-choice and short-answer questions enable the students to self-assess.

A marking grid is included on page 105 to help parents or teachers keep track of the kinds of questions students are having difficulty with in the mixed questions text. The grid provides a useful visual record for diagnostic and remediation purposes.

Tips

- Record each student's results. Use the marking grid to record the results for the mixed questions section.
- Assess students' results. Analyse the patterns of correct and incorrect answers in students' results to identify areas of strength and weakness to assist with further development. Use this information to target and revise areas that need further attention.
- Identify the kinds of comprehension questions students are having difficulty with. Students for whom English is an additional language or dialect (EAL/D) often have most difficulty with inferring types of questions and questions which require background knowledge, or which use idioms that native speakers of English grow up using or knowing. English idioms can cause problems for many students, but especially students for whom English is a second language. Comprehension questions that depend on these concepts and ideas are specifically taught in the language questions section of this book.

Types of texts

The texts included in this book are defined according to their purposes: informative, imaginative and persuasive. Extracts from classic texts have been chosen to support the Australian Curriculum English Literature strand. Texts have also been chosen to support General Capabilities (Ethical Behaviour, Intercultural Understanding) and Cross-curricular Priorities (Aboriginal and Torres Strait Islander Histories and Cultures, Sustainability, Asia and Australia's engagement with Asia) of the Australian Curriculum.

Reading strategies

The following strategies can help you improve your reading.

1 Skimming

What is it? **Skimming** is a way to have a quick first look at a text.

How do you do it? Move your eyes quickly over the text. Or zig zag across and down. Stop briefly at parts that get your attention, such as headings and illustrations. Notice features such as the layout, paragraphs, columns, bullet points, photos, diagrams, labels and use of colour. These things can give you clues about the text and its purpose and audience.

2 Visualising

What is it? **Visualising** is making pictures in your mind as you read. Visualising as you read helps you remember what you have read. It helps you 'see' what you are reading about.

How do you do it? You picture in your mind what is described in a text. For example, you could imagine what characters or an imaginary animal in a story look like from their descriptions.

3 Connecting

What is it? **Connecting** is making connections with the text. Connecting with the ideas in a text helps you understand the text and remember what it's about.

How do you do it? Think about the text and how it relates to you and your life as you read. For example, 'This reminds me of …', 'I've been to a place like that' or 'I don't agree with that'.

4 Predicting

What is it? **Predicting** is thinking ahead as you read and making guesses about the text.

How do you do it? As you read you use evidence in the text to make predictions. For example, you can predict what might happen next in a story. As you read on you can confirm your predictions. You can also change your predictions based on new evidence in the text.

⑤ Inferring

What is it? Inferring is working out what is meant in a text when the information is not directly stated. Inferring means reading between the lines.

How do you do it? As you read you use the evidence in the text to work out what is implied.

⑥ Monitoring

What is it? Monitoring is making sure that what you read makes sense to you.

How do you do it? When you monitor your reading you notice when meaning is lost. You re-read that section of the text or scan back over the text to see where meaning broke down. You correct your understanding of the text so that it makes sense to you.

⑦ Judging

What is it? Judging is forming opinions as you read. Making judgements as you read makes you a more effective reader.

How do you do it? As you read you make judgements about the text. For example, you can judge the purpose of the text and the ideas in it. You can judge the values and opinions of the writer and you can make judgements about the audience for the text.

⑧ Scanning

What is it? Scanning is looking over a text to search for particular information. When you scan you don't need to read the whole text. You only read or re-read the parts of the text you need.

How do you do it? Look quickly over the text. Search for particular words, phrases or images. For example, you can scan a table of contents to find a page number. You can scan a class photo for your image or you can scan a graph to find the details you need.

Step-by-step guide to reading texts

This part of the **Step-by-step guide** shows you what to do when reading a text.

STEP 1

Skim the text.

Think.

- **Skim** over the text.
- Look at how it is set out. Look at any illustrations and other visual elements.
- **Read** the title.
- **Predict** what the text might be about.
- **Predict** the purpose of the text.

Skim

Predict

STEP 2

Read the text.

Think about the text.

- **Visualise** or form mental pictures as you read.
- **Monitor** your reading.
- Make sure you understand what you are reading. **Re-read** the parts you don't understand.

Visualise

Monitor

- **Connect** with the ideas in the text. **Think** about what you already know about the subject and the type of text.

Connect

- Use clues in the text to **infer** meaning. **Think** and make **judgements**.

Infer

Judge

This part of the **Step-by-step guide** shows you how to answer questions about a text.

STEP 3		
Read the question. **Think** about what type of question it is.	Decide whether the question is: ✪ fact-finding ✪ synthesis ✪ inferring ✪ language ✪ judgement.	✪ **Think** about the question and what you remember about the text.

STEP 4 **Work out** what you need to do to answer the question.

Fact-finding	✪ Find the answer.	✪ **Scan** the text to find the relevant parts. **Re-read** parts or the whole text to find the answer.
Synthesis	✪ Connect ideas and information.	✪ **Scan** the text to find the relevant parts. **Re-read** parts or the whole text if necessary, and connect information to draw conclusions.
Inferring	✪ Read between the lines.	✪ **Scan** the text for the relevant parts. **Re-read** parts or the whole text if necessary. Read between the lines to infer meaning.
Language	✪ Work out how language is used.	✪ **Scan** the text for the relevant parts. **Re-read** parts or the whole text if necessary. Use your knowledge of how language works at the paragraph, sentence, clause and word level.
Judgement	✪ Make judgements.	✪ **Scan** the text for the relevant parts. **Re-read** parts or the whole text if necessary. **Think** critically. Use your own knowledge and understanding.

Scan

TYPES OF QUESTIONS

Step-by-step guide to fact-finding questions

To answer **fact-finding** questions you need to find the answer in the text.

Use this **Step-by-step** guide to help you read the text and **find facts** to answer the questions below. Circle the correct answers or write your answer on the line.

STEP 1	**Skim** the text. **Think**.	✪ **Skim** over the text. Look at how it is set out. Look at the illustration. **Think** about what the illustration shows you. **Read** the title, *Bushfire survival plan.* **Predict** what the text might be about.
STEP 2	**Read** the text. **Think**. Does it make sense to you?	✪ **Monitor** your reading. ✪ **Think**. What do you know about the subject?

Bushfire survival plan

Bushfires can be a risk for people in cities and towns as well as people in the bush. Fire services give the weather a Fire Danger Rating or FDR. The FDR tells you if fire danger is a big risk that day or only a low risk that day. The worst fire danger rating is catastrophic.

Everyone should have a bushfire survival plan. A bushfire survival plan is a list of things you will do if there's a bushfire. You need to make sure that every member of your family knows about the plan and what to do if there's a bushfire.

Question 1 What is a bushfire survival plan?

A a plan to leave your home
B a list of what to do if there's a bushfire
C a plan for fighting a bushfire

STEP 3	**Read** the question. Work out what type of question it is.	✪ This is a **fact-finding** question. **Think** about what you have **read. Think** about what a bushfire survival plan is.

STEP 4	Work out how to answer the question.	✪ **Scan** the text for the words *bushfire survival plan* to find what a bushfire survival plan is.

Answer: B is correct. The answer is a fact in the text. You read *A bushfire survival plan is a list of things you will do if there's a bushfire (see lines 7–9).* **A** and **C** are incorrect. The text does not state that a bushfire survival plan is a plan to leave your home or a plan for fighting a bushfire.

Question 2 What is an FDR?

A Fire Disaster Record B Fiery Dragon Risk C Fire Danger Rating

STEP 3	**Read** the question. Work out what type of question it is.	✪ This is a **fact-finding** question. **Think** about what you have read in the text. **Think** about what an FDR is.
STEP 4	Work out how to answer the question.	✪ **Scan** the text for the letters *FDR* to find out what they stand for.

Answer: C is correct. The answer is a fact in the text. You read *Fire services give the weather a Fire Danger Rating or FDR (see lines 3–4).* **A** and **B** are incorrect as these are not what the text says. You should also use common sense to work out that **B** is incorrect as it is not a sensible option in a factual text.

Question 3 Who needs to know about your bushfire plan?

A fire services B every family member C everyone

STEP 3	**Read** the question. Work out what type of question it is.	✪ This is a **fact-finding** question. **Think** about what you have **read**. **Think** about who the text says needs to know about your plan.
STEP 4	Work out how to answer the question.	✪ **Scan** the text for words that tell who needs to know about your plan.

Answer: B is correct. The answer is a fact in the text. You read *You need to make sure that every member of your family knows about the plan (see lines 9–10).* **A** and **C** are incorrect. Only your family members need to know about your plan.

Question 4 What is the worst fire rating?

....

STEP 3	**Read** the question. Work out what type of question it is.	✪ This is a **fact-finding** question. **Think** about what you have **read. Think** about the worst fire rating.
STEP 4	Work out how to answer the question.	✪ **Scan** the text and illustration for the words *worst fire rating.*

Answer: The answer is *catastrophic*. You read *The worst fire danger rating is catastrophic (see line 6).*

Now write!

Write your family's bushfire survival plan.

Note: The text is informative—a report. It uses technical terminology and factual information.

Fact-finding questions

Use the **Step-by-step guide** on pages 8–9 to help you read the text and **find facts** to answer the questions below. Circle the correct answers or write your answer on the line.

New | Reply | Delete | Archive | Junk | Sweep | Move to

School holidays

Hi Nan

I can't wait till the holidays. Mum says we'll drive up Saturday. I can stay with you the whole two weeks. Mum and Dad will only stay for the weekend. Then Dad will come back to get me on the Sunday before school goes back.

Can we do more cooking? Can we make scones again? I loved them last time. Mum wants me to make and freeze some for her.

View online   Download as zip

Can we also make the boiled pineapple fruit cake? Dad likes that best. He likes to take a piece to work every day. I told him how much fruit was in it and that it had very little sugar. He says it must be good for his health. I told him that cake is a sometime food. He laughed.

Love Ellie

PS Do you like the photo?

1. How long will Ellie stay with Nan?
   - **A** Sunday
   - **B** two weeks
   - **C** the weekend
2. When will Dad drive back to collect Ellie?
   - **A** Saturday
   - **B** the Sunday before school goes back
   - **C** after the weekend
3. What kind of cake does Dad like?
   - **A** fruit cake
   - **B** a sometime food
   - **C** scones
4. What activity does Ellie like to do with Nan?
   - **A** taking photos
   - **B** going to the beach
   - **C** cooking
5. What ingredients are used to make Nan's fruit cake?
   - **A** fruit
   - **B** very little sugar
   - **C** fruit and sugar
6. How is Ellie getting to her Nan's?

   ....

Now write!

Write an email to a family member. Attach a photo. Tell the person what you have been doing or about your plans.

Note: This is an informative text—an email. The writer gives her personal opinions. The text uses personal pronouns.

Answers and explanations on p. 82

Fact-finding questions

Use the **Step-by-step guide** on pages 8–9 to help you read the text and **find facts** to answer the questions below. Circle the correct answers or write your answer on the lines.

Not for sale

Why did you write that note, Steven?

I don't want anyone to buy our house.

I don't either. Do you think the note will work?

It might. I'm going to leave it out for people to see when they come to look over our house.

Mum and Dad had better not see it.

You can help me, Lou. We can keep watch and hide it from Mum and Dad after the people have left.

We'll really get into trouble if Mum and Dad see it.

It'll be worth it if the note stops people buying our house. I love living on this island.

Me too. I don't want to move to the city.

> Dear People
>
> Please don't buy our island home. We don't want to move.
>
> Signed Steven Short

1. Who wrote the note?
   A Dad
   B Lou
   C Steven

2. The note asks people
   A not to buy their house.
   B to buy their house.
   C to sell their house.

3. How does Steven think Lou can help him?
   A by hiding the note
   B by telling their Mum and Dad about the note
   C by keeping watch and hiding the note from Mum and Dad

4. Where do Steven and Lou live?
   A in the city
   B on an island
   C in the suburbs

5. What does Lou think will happen if Mum and Dad see the note?
   A Steven will get into trouble.
   B Steven and Lou will get into trouble.
   C Mum and Dad will understand.

6. Why doesn't Steven want people to buy the house?

   ....

   ....

   ....

Now write!

Write a note or write a conversation about something you don't want to happen.

Note: The texts are persuasive. One is a conversation. It has direct speech, questions, statements and personal opinions. The other is a note. It gives an opinion and a command.

Answers and explanations on p. 82

Fact-finding questions

Use the **Step-by-step guide** on pages 8–9 to help you read the text and **find facts** to answer the questions below. Circle the correct answers or write your answer on the lines.

The visitor

Last year, at Christmas time, our family rented a holiday house. It was on a hill near the sea. There was a large area of bush beside the house.

One morning I looked out of the window and saw that there was something on the driveway. It hadn't been there yesterday. It looked like a long, diamond-patterned rope. It stretched from the bottom to the top of the driveway.

I was going to have a better look but Dad told me to stay inside.

'That's a python on our driveway,' he told the family. 'Leave it alone. It will go back into the bush when it's ready. We'll call Parks and Wildlife tomorrow if it's still there when we need to use the car.'

1. When did the family rent a holiday house?
   - **A** in the morning
   - **B** last Christmas
   - **C** yesterday
2. What was beside the house?
   - **A** a hill
   - **B** the sea
   - **C** an area of bush
3. What did the snake look like?
   - **A** something on the driveway
   - **B** a rope
   - **C** diamonds
4. How far did the 'rope' stretch?
   - **A** from the bottom to the top of the driveway
   - **B** across the driveway
   - **C** from the driveway to the house
5. Where did the narrator's Dad tell him or her to stay?
   - **A** inside
   - **B** at the window
   - **C** on the driveway
6. What did Dad tell the family to do about the python?

   ....

   ....

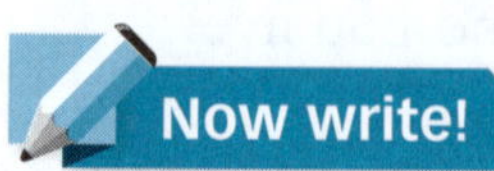

Now write!

Write about an event that gave you a surprise. Tell what happened and say why it made you surprised.

Note: The text is informative—a recount. It includes a personal response.

Answers and explanations on pp. 82–83

Fact-finding questions

Use the **Step-by-step guide** on pages 8–9 to help you read the text and **find facts** to answer the questions below. Circle the correct answers or write your answer on the line.

Tango Times, 3 July

Brush turkey thinks it's a chicken

Young schoolboy Max Wong had a surprise for our local reporter, Sarah Simms. Max told her a brush turkey that thinks it's a chicken lives at his place.

'When it was very small it waddled into our back yard,' Max said. 'It had brown feathers and looked like a little duck.'

Soon the baby brush turkey was living in the hen house. When the chickens were fed, the baby brush turkey pecked up its share. When the hens roosted, the small fluffy ball roosted as well.

Max explained that as it became an adult, the brush turkey's appearance changed completely.

'But the chickens think it is just another chicken,' he grinned. 'We call it Bruce.'

1. What is the brush turkey's name?
   - A Max
   - B Sarah
   - C Bruce
2. What did the brush turkey look like as a baby?
   - A a little duck
   - B a little chicken
   - C a baby turkey
3. Where does the baby brush turkey live?
   - A in the house
   - B in the garden
   - C in the hen house
4. The baby brush turkey ____________ the chicken's food.
   - A pecked
   - B chewed
   - C gobbled
5. What happened to the baby brush turkey as it became an adult?
   - A It turned into a chicken.
   - B Its appearance changed.
   - C It learned how to roost.
6. What does Max say the chickens think the brush turkey is?

   ....

Now write!

Write a report for your local newspaper about an animal that behaves in a surprising way. Include a headline for your report.

Note: The text is informative—a newspaper article. It gives an amusing account about an animal's actions.

Answers and explanations on p. 83

Fact-finding questions

Use the **Step-by-step guide** on pages 8–9 to help you read the text and **find facts** to answer the questions below. Circle the correct answers or write your answer on the lines.

Historic houses | Events | Stories | Contact us

Our virtual tour

Our class went on a virtual tour yesterday. A virtual tour means we went on the tour using a computer rather than in real life. We clicked on a website for historic houses. Then we clicked on an icon that took us on our virtual tour.

There was a guide who talked about the historic houses we were shown through. Most of the houses were big and built well over a hundred years ago. The kitchens had lots of old-fashioned cooking equipment for the servants to use. The gardens looked amazing.

In the upstairs bedrooms, the beds looked much higher than the beds we have today. There were steps beside some of them. The guide said that some people needed the steps to climb into their beds!

We all enjoyed our virtual tour.

1 Which virtual tour website did the class use?
- A houses
- B historic houses
- C virtual tours

2 Who talked about the houses on the website?
- A a teacher
- B a class member
- C a guide

3 Most of the houses were built
- A in modern times.
- B over a hundred years ago.
- C a short time ago.

4 What size were the houses?
- A old-fashioned
- B big
- C amazing

5 The beds in the historic houses were
- A higher than the beds of today.
- B lower than the beds of today.
- C the same size as the beds of today.

6 Why did some people need steps in their bedrooms?

....

....

Now write!

Write about a place you have visited with your class. Say where you went, how you got there, what you saw and what you did.

Note: The text is informative—a recount. It uses the past tense to tell about events that have happened.

Answers and explanations on p. 83

Fact-finding questions

Use the **Step-by-step guide** on pages 8–9 to help you read the text and **find facts** to answer the questions below. Circle the correct answers or write your answer on the lines.

Dugongs

Dugongs are marine mammals. They come to the surface to breathe air but they can remain under water for up to six minutes. Dugongs can grow up to 3.5 metres long. Most of the world's dugongs live off the coast of Australia.

Dugongs eat the seagrass that grows in warm shallow sea water. Dugongs are often called sea cows because they graze on grass in seabed meadows.

Dugongs are a vulnerable species. Vulnerable means they are in danger of becoming extinct. One reason they are vulnerable is because they mainly eat seagrass. When seagrass dies dugongs starve. Seagrass dies when water gets polluted. Many dugongs are killed or hurt when boats run into them. They also die when they get tangled in fishing nets.

1 How long can dugongs remain under water?

- A up to ten minutes
- B up to six minutes
- C more than ten minutes

2 What do dugongs eat?

- A They graze.
- B They eat fish.
- C They eat seagrass.

3 Where are most of the world's dugongs?

- A swimming
- B off the coast of Australia
- C in sea water

4 Why do dugongs come to the surface?

- A to find other dugongs
- B to breathe air
- C to find seagrass beds

5 Where does seagrass grow?

- A in warm water
- B in the sea
- C in warm shallow sea water

6 Why do dugongs starve?

....

....

....

Now write!

Research an animal. Write a report. Include information about what sort of creature it is, where it lives, what it looks like, what it eats and any threats it faces. Include an illustration.

Note: The text is informative—a report. It includes technical terminology and facts.

Answers and explanations on p. 83

Fact-finding questions

Use the **Step-by-step guide** on pages 8–9 to help you read the text and **find facts** to answer the questions below. Circle the correct answers or write your answer on the line.

HELP WANTED

Position: TROLL HUNTER

The Village of Hartford needs help with the terrible troll that lives under our Hartford Shire Bridge. Our villagers are too frightened to use the bridge. The troll is eating our goats.

We seek a brave person who will take the troll away. We don't want to harm the troll. We want it taken away to a better home such as a cave, far away.

Applications for the job of Troll Hunter should be sent to: Post Office Manager, Hartford

PLEASE include details of past troll-hunting jobs.

NOTE: Hartford is a gun-free village.

1. Where does the troll live?
   - **A** on Hartford Shire Bridge
   - **B** under Hartford Shire Bridge
   - **C** in a cave
2. What do the Hartford villagers want?
   - **A** the troll taken away
   - **B** the troll killed
   - **C** the troll captured
3. Why is the troll a problem?
   - **A** It eats villagers and goats.
   - **B** It eats goats.
   - **C** It eats goats and blocks the bridge.
4. Where should applications be sent?
   - **A** to the Village of Hartford
   - **B** to the Post Office Manager
   - **C** to the Hartford police station
5. What sort of person should apply for the job?
   - **A** the Post Office Manager
   - **B** a brave man
   - **C** any brave man or woman
6. Where is a better home for the troll?

   ....

Now write!

Create a 'Help wanted' poster for a nursery rhyme or folktale of your choice. For example, you might ask for help to build safer houses for the three little pigs. Or you might ask for help from jigsaw puzzle experts to put Humpty Dumpty together again.

Note: The text is imaginative—a poster. It uses the characters and ideas from the folktale *The Three Billy Goats Gruff.*

Answers and explanations on pp. 83–84

Fact-finding questions

Use the **Step-by-step guide** on pages 8–9 to help you read the text and **find facts** to answer the questions below. Circle the correct answers or write your answer on the line.

Invisibility potion

WARNING! Only use once a week or the effect becomes permanent (You will be invisible forever!).

This potion allows the user to become invisible for exactly 60 minutes.

Note: clothing will not become invisible so you will need to remove it. Watch the time or you will find yourself visible again and naked.

INGREDIENTS

1 tablespoon grass tree nectar

2 tablespoons blue flax lily juice

1 cup roasted rock lily stems

2 cups crushed lilly pilly fruit

½ cup ground wattle seeds

METHOD

Mix all ingredients.

Roll mixture into 1 cm balls.

Store in airtight container in refrigerator.

INSTRUCTION

Chew and swallow 1 ball to become instantly invisible. Effect lasts exactly 60 minutes.

1 Why should you only use the potion once a week?
  - A The effect becomes permanent.
  - B You become invisible for 60 minutes.
  - C It won't work properly.

2 What happens 60 minutes after taking the potion?
  - A You become invisible.
  - B You become naked.
  - C You will be visible.

3 Where do you keep the potion?
  - A in a safe place
  - B in a fridge
  - C in balls

4 How much of the potion should you take to become invisible?
  - A Chew and swallow all ingredients.
  - B Take one ball.
  - C Take it once a week.

5 Why do you need to take off your clothes?
  - A so you are naked
  - B so you look funny
  - C because they won't become invisible

6 Which ingredient needs to be cooked before use?

....

Now write!

Create a recipe for a potion that gives you magical powers, such as the ability to fly or to walk through or see through walls. Or imagine that you swallowed some of the invisibility potion. Write a story about your adventures.

Note: The text is imaginative—a recipe. The text uses humour. It includes warnings and commands.

Answers and explanations on p. 84

Step-by-step guide to synthesis questions

To answer **synthesis** questions you need to connect ideas and information from across the text.

Use this **Step-by-step guide** to help you read the text and **synthesise** information to answer the questions below. Circle the correct answers or write your answers on the line or in the boxes.

STEP (1)	**Skim** the text. **Think**.	**Skim** over the text. Look at how it is set out. Notice that it is in paragraphs. **Think** about what the illustration shows you. **Read** the title, *Making milk*. **Predict** what the text might be about.
STEP (2)	**Read** the text. **Think**. Does the text make sense to you?	**Re-read** the parts that you don't understand. **Think**. What do you know about the subject?

Making milk

A dairy cow makes about 25 to 30 litres of milk a day. To do this it needs to eat about 40 kilograms of grasses and fodder. It also needs to drink at least half a bath full of water.

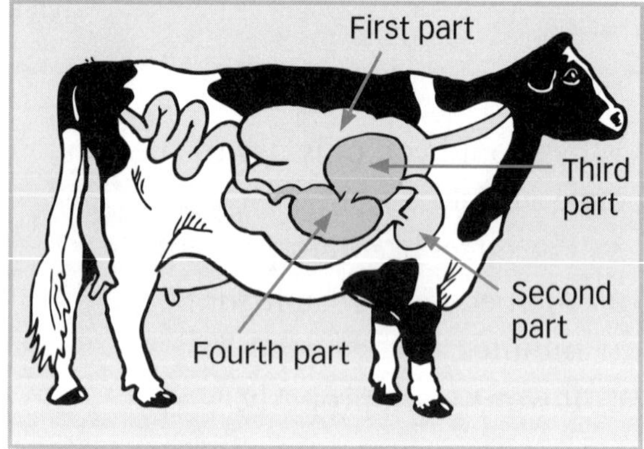

A cow's stomach has four parts. The first part softens the food. The second part turns the food into small balls or cuds. Then the cuds are returned to the mouth for more chewing.

The cud is swallowed and goes to the third and fourth parts of the stomach. There the nutrients from the grass are turned into milk by four mammary glands in the udder.

Question 1 What is the purpose of paragraph one?

A to describe a cow's stomach B to introduce the topic C to explain how milk is made

STEP (3)	**Read** the question. Work out what type of question it is.	This is a **synthesis** question. **Think** about the information in paragraph one.
STEP (4)	Work out how to answer the question.	**Re-read** paragraph one. **Think** about the purpose of this information in the text.

Answer: B is correct. The information in paragraph one introduces the topic of what dairy cows eat and drink to make milk. **A** is incorrect. The cow's stomach is described in paragraph two. **C** is incorrect because how milk is made is described in paragraph three.

Question 2 Write the numbers 1 to 3 in the boxes to show the order of events.

☐ The cow chews cud. ☐ The cow makes milk. ☐ The cow swallows food.

STEP 3	**Read** the question. Work out what type of question it is.	✪ This is a **synthesis** question. **Think** about the order of events in the text.
STEP 4	Work out how to answer the question.	✪ **Re-read** the parts of the text which tell you the order in which the cow chews cud, makes milk and swallows food.

Answer: 2, 3, 1. The cow has to swallow the food (1) then chew the cud (2) before it is able to make milk (3).

Question 3 The diagram shows

A how a cow makes milk.
B the four parts of a cow's stomach.
C all the organs inside a cow.

STEP 3	**Read** the question. Work out what type of question it is.	✪ This is a **synthesis** question. **Think** about what you have read and what the diagram shows.
STEP 4	Work out how to answer the question.	✪ **Re-read** the labels on the diagram. **Re-read** the text to work out how the information in the diagram connects to the text.

Answer: **B is correct.** The diagram shows the parts of the cow's stomach that are used to make milk. **A** is incorrect because the diagram does not show how a cow makes milk. **C** is incorrect because the diagram doesn't show all of a cow's organs, such as its heart and lungs.

Question 4 Write a different title for the text.

....

STEP 3	**Read** the question. Work out what type of question it is.	✪ This is a **synthesis** question. **Think** about what you have **read** across the whole text.
STEP 4	Work out how to answer the question.	✪ **Think** what the whole text is about. Think of a title that suits all the information in the text.

Answer: Your title will be about cows and/or the way the food they eat becomes milk. For example, it could be 'Dairy cows' or 'How cows make milk'.

Now write!

Research how something is made (e.g. jam or paper). Write an explanation.

Note: The text is informative—an explanation. It uses technical terms. It uses a diagram with labels.

Synthesis questions

Use the **Step-by-step guide** on pages 18–19 to help you read the text and **synthesise** information to answer the questions below. Circle the correct answers or write your answer on the lines.

Try gymnastics

My name is Anna. I love to do gymnastics. I recommend gymnastics to other children.

The reasons are:

- It is good fun.
- It is good exercise.
- It makes me strong.
- It improves my balance and coordination.
- My class does tumbling and trampolining.
- My class uses good music.
- Lots of my friends do gymnastics too.

These are all the reasons I love gymnastics.

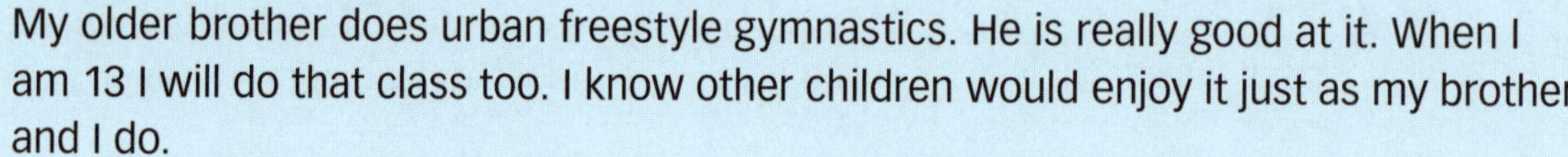

My older brother does urban freestyle gymnastics. He is really good at it. When I am 13 I will do that class too. I know other children would enjoy it just as my brother and I do.

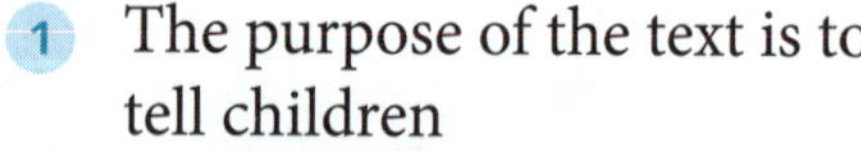

1 The purpose of the text is to tell children

A how to do gymnastics.

B to try gymnastics.

C what gymnastics is.

2 The main idea in the text is that Anna

A likes to keep fit.

B has friends at gymnastics.

C enjoys gymnastics.

3 Which statement could belong in Anna's list of reasons?

A It makes me more flexible.

B Classes are held after school.

C I do three classes a week.

4 Why does Anna recommend gymnastics?

A Her brother does it.

B Other children enjoy it.

C It is good exercise.

5 Which idea is not about health?

A It improves my balance and coordination.

B My class has tumbling and trampolining.

C My class uses good music.

6 Who has Anna written the text for?

....

....

Now write!

Write a list of recommendations about a hobby or sport that you enjoy. Write for children your own age. Recommend the activity to them.

Note: The text is persuasive—a recommendation. It gives personal opinions in a logical order. It uses persuasive devices and evaluative language.

Answers and explanations on p. 84

Synthesis questions

Use the **Step-by-step guide** on pages 18–19 to help you read the text and **synthesise** information to answer the questions below. Circle the correct answers or write your answers on the lines or in the boxes.

> Club news | Seasons | About us | Contact us
>
> **COME FRUIT-PICKING**
>
> Persuade your family to come fruit-picking. Have a picnic on our farm. FREE entry. Pay only for what you pick.
>
> Grab a bucket. Fill it up with fresh fruit you pick yourself. Fruit dripping with juice-licking goodness. Eat it there and then. And take some home for healthy, delicious treats. Click here for recipes.
>
> Choose from mouth-watering cherries, raspberries, peaches or strawberries.
>
> Our company, Fruit-pickers, has orchards all over Australia. Type your postcode here [ ] to find your nearest fruit-picking farm.
>
> Click here for information about fruit-picking seasons.
>
> Contact us   Join our Friends of Fruit-pickers club for free.

1. The purpose of this website is to
   - **A** persuade families to pick fruit at Fruit-pickers.
   - **B** invite people to join Friends of Fruit-pickers.
   - **C** explain how to pick strawberries.

2. Where in the text could you add this information?

   Freeze the fruit for future treats.
   - **A** just before *Persuade your family* ...
   - **B** after *delicious treats* ...
   - **C** after *Have a picnic on our farm.*

3. Which information is **not** available on this website?
   - **A** information about fruit-picking seasons
   - **B** where to find Fruit-pickers' orchards
   - **C** the health benefits of different fruits

4. What is the main message in the text?
   - **A** Entry is free.
   - **B** Freshly picked fruit is delicious.
   - **C** Fruit-picking is hard work.

5. Number these actions from 1 to 4 in the order you would do them.
   - ☐ Take some fruit home.
   - ☐ Eat the fruit.
   - ☐ Pick the fruit.
   - ☐ Enter the farm.

6. How do you find recipes?

   ....

   ....

Design a web page that persuades people to buy a product.

Note: The text is persuasive—an online advertisement. It uses persuasive words and tevaluative language.

Answers and explanations on pp. 84–85

Synthesis questions

Use the **Step-by-step guide** on pages 18–19 to help you read the text and **synthesise** information to answer the questions below. Circle the correct answers or write your answers on the lines.

Our experiment

My class did a fun experiment.

First we poured three quarters of a cup of water into a small, clear plastic bottle. Then we filled the bottle almost to the top with vegetable oil. The oil floated on top of the water.

Next we added 10 drops of food colouring. We watched our green food colouring go through the oil and down to the water to colour it. Then we added half a fizzy* tablet.

The tablet sank to the bottom and started to fizz. Then the fizzy gas bubbles rose to the top of the oil. They carried green water to the top with them. The gas bubbles burst at the top and then the green water sank back down through the oil. It looked good.

We learned that gas is lighter than oil and oil is lighter than water.

*The fizzy tablet is medicine adults sometimes use for an upset stomach.

1. What is the purpose of the text?
   - A to tell a story
   - B to give instructions
   - C to tell what happened
2. The writer thinks the activity was
   - A fun but a waste of time.
   - B fun and interesting.
   - C fun but it didn't work very well.
3. What did the food colouring do?
   - A It made the bottle look pretty.
   - B It coloured the oil.
   - C It showed how the fizzy gas rose through the oil.
4. Where might you find a text like this?
   - A in a school newsletter
   - B in a newspaper
   - C in a science book in the library
5. Would the experiment work with red food colouring?

   ....

6. Does this photo match the text? Explain.

....

....

....

Now write!

Write a recount about a class activity that you enjoyed. It might have been an art lesson, a maths activity or a game that you played.

Note: The text is informative—a recount. It uses time order (*First … next …*) to sequence information. It uses technical terminology.

Answers and explanations on p. 85

Synthesis questions

Use the **Step-by-step guide** on pages 18–19 to help you read the text and **synthesise** information to answer the questions below. Circle the correct answers or write your answers on the line or in the boxes.

Book review

Book title: *The Treasure Box*

Author: Margaret Wild; Illustrator: Freya Blackwood

The Treasure Box is a really good book. It is about a boy called Peter and his father. Their city is bombed and the library is destroyed. Only one library book is saved from the bombs because Peter's father has it at home.

Peter and his father flee the city. They put the book in an iron box and take it with them. Peter's father says the book is their treasure. He says "It is rarer than rubies, more splendid than silver, greater than gold." He makes Peter promise to keep the treasure safe.

All the people from the city walk for days and days. When Peter can't carry it any more he buries the iron box under a tree. Then, years later when he has grown up, he finds the tree and digs up the treasure. He gives it to a library so everyone can read it.

I think it's good that a book is the treasure. I like the illustrations too.

By Jian, Year 2

1. What is the text mainly about?
   - A Peter and his father
   - B a book that Jian read
   - C a box of treasure
2. Why do Peter and his father flee the city?
   - A The library was destroyed.
   - B They walk for days and days.
   - C The city was bombed.
3. What else might a reader want to know about the book *The Treasure Box*?
   - A What is the treasure?
   - B How did Peter find the right tree?
   - C Was the treasure kept safe?
4. Write the numbers 1 to 3 in the boxes to show the order of events in *The Treasure Box*.
   - ☐ Peter dug up the treasure.
   - ☐ The city was bombed.
   - ☐ Peter promised to look after the treasure.
5. Choose a different title to suit the book.
   - A Buried Treasure
   - B Peter Finds a Treasure
   - C A Treasure to Share
6. Why does Jian like *The Treasure Box*?

   ....

Now write!

Choose a book that you have enjoyed. Write a review that recommends it to others.

Note: The text is persuasive—a book review.

Answers and explanations on p. 85

Synthesis questions

Use the **Step-by-step guide** on pages 18–19 to help you read the text and **synthesise** information to answer the questions below. Circle the correct answers or write your answer on the lines.

My hair

I'd like a different hair style,
Some stripes of pink or green.
Or maybe have some dreadlocks,
Or add a sparkly sheen.

My hair's so hard to manage:
It likes to turn and flounce.
If only I could tame it,
Get rid of all its bounce.

Of course I could just grow it
Until it's very long,
Or choose a really short cut.
That way I'd not go wrong.

Dad says I need a mohawk
That sticks up high and straight.
Mum says No! She loves my hair.
Mmm. P'raps I'd better wait.

by Katy

1 In the poem Katy thinks mainly about
- **A** ways to change her hair.
- **B** different hair colours.
- **C** what others think about her hair.

2 Which is the first change of hairstyle Katy thinks of trying?
- **A** cutting her hair short
- **B** getting coloured stripes
- **C** growing her hair long

3 What problem does Katy write about in stanza 2?
- **A** colouring her hair
- **B** controlling her hair
- **C** cutting her hair

4 Choose a different title for this poem.
- **A** Katy needs a haircut
- **B** Katy wants a mohawk
- **C** Will I, won't I?

5 Katy's parents
- **A** disagree with Katy about her hair.
- **B** disagree with each other about Katy's hair.
- **C** agree with each other about Katy's hair.

6 Why does Katy decide not to change her hair just yet?

....

....

....

Now write!

Write a poem in the first person. It could be, for example, about deciding what kind of pet you'd like or what you want to be when you grow up.

Note: The text is imaginative—a poem. It has a first-person narrator. It presents the narrator's point of view and uses evaluative language. It is written in stanzas with lines that rhyme.

Answers and explanations on p. 85

Synthesis questions

Use the **Step-by-step guide** on pages 18–19 to help you read the text and **synthesise** information to answer the questions below. Circle the correct answers or write your answer on the lines.

Testing, testing

Prince Ferdy didn't want a princess for his wife. He wanted a normal, easy-going girl.

He remembered how his brother, Prince Basil, had chosen his wife. He'd invited his girlfriend to the family home and used the three peas under the mattresses test. She couldn't sleep a wink. She was so delicate. She was a *real* princess. She became his wife.

Ferdy decided to use the same test but with a twist of his own. He invited his girlfriend to the family home. He put a bunch of carrots, some celery and a box of apples under her mattresses instead of the three peas.

'Sleep well?' Ferdy asked next morning.

'Like a log,' Ferdy's girlfriend smiled.

Ferdy proposed. They both lived happily ever after.

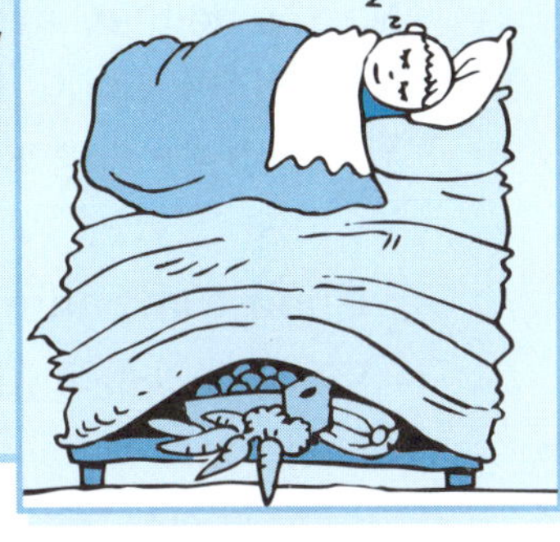

1. Ferdy and Basil like
   - A different types of mattress.
   - B different types of girl.
   - C different types of food.
2. What is the lesson or moral of the story?
   - A Never marry a princess.
   - B An apple a day keeps the doctor away.
   - C Always make your own choices.
3. Which happened first?
   - A Ferdy decided who to marry.
   - B Ferdy thought of a twist to the test.
   - C Ferdy's girlfriend slept on the fruit and vegetables.
4. What did Ferdy's test prove?
   - A that his girlfriend is easy going
   - B that the test is useless
   - C that his girlfriend is a princess
5. What is the purpose of the text?
   - A to give instructions for a special test
   - B to entertain
   - C to teach princes how to find wives
6. What might have happened if Prince Ferdy had agreed to marry a wife like Prince Basil's? Explain.

   ....

   ....

   ....

   ....

Now write!

Write a story about a Princess and her test to find the right husband.

Note: The text is imaginative—a narrative. It is based on the fairy tale *The Princess and the Pea* by Hans Christian Anderson, 1835. The text uses quotation marks, question and answer, and the past tense. It implies a moral or a lesson.

Answers and explanations on p. 86

Synthesis questions

Use the **Step-by-step guide** on pages 18–19 to help you read the text and **synthesise** information to answer the questions below. Circle the correct answers or write your answer in the box.

Cockroaches

'Cockroaches are disgusting,' said David. 'They spread disease.'

'Not all of them,' protested Selina. 'Australia has hundreds of native cockroaches. They live in the bush. They are important in the food web.'

'Really?' asked David. He wasn't convinced.

'Yes. It's true. Native cockroaches are good. They are food for frogs, birds, reptiles and little mammals. That's important! And they do other things to help nature.'

'Well, I still don't like cockroaches in my house.'

'No, me neither,' agreed Selina. 'Cockroaches you find at home are species from other parts of the world. Those ones don't belong here.'

'Yes. They're disgusting,' said David.

1 Choose an ending for this sentence:
Some people don't know that native cockroaches

A are pests.
B are good for the environment.
C eat frogs.

2 Choose a different title for the text.

A Spreading disease
B The food web
C Defending cockroaches

3 *'Cockroaches are disgusting,' said David* (line 2). David said this

A to start an argument.
B to give an opinion.
C to describe cockroaches.

4 What is the main idea in the text?

A Nobody likes cockroaches.
B You should rid your home of cockroaches.
C Some cockroaches are useful.

5 How are Selina and David's opinions the same?

A They dislike cockroaches in their homes.
B They both worry about germs.
C They agree that cockroaches are useful.

6 Write the numbers from the box in the columns.

(1) spread disease
(2) are part of the food web
(3) are pests
(4) are important
(5) live in the bush
(6) live in people's homes

Cockroaches in the home	Cockroaches in the bush

Now write!

Write a conversation between two people who have strong opinions about a topic of your choice. Use speech marks for what each person says. Use saying verbs.

Note: The text is persuasive—a conversation. It includes opinions and evaluative language (*disgusting*). It uses quotation marks and saying verbs (*said, protested, asked*).

Answers and explanations on p. 86

Synthesis questions

Use the **Step-by-step guide** on pages 18–19 to help you read the text and **synthesise** information to answer the questions below. Circle the correct answers or write your answer on the lines.

Sharks

Poem 1

Killing machine
Monster shark—
cold blood and dead eyes.
Sharp teeth
rip
through flesh
to kill.
Sneaky,
silent
man-eater.
Terrifying!

Poem 2

Sleek beauty
Great white
gracefully gliding.
Top predator:
does not kill for sport.
Important in the web of life.
Wondrous fish
belongs in the ocean.
At home—
roaming the seas.
Magnificent!

© Tanya Dalgleish

1. What is the main message in Poem 1?
   - **A** Sharks are deadly killers.
   - **B** Sharks are sneaky.
   - **C** Sharks have sharp teeth.
2. What is the main message in Poem 2?
   - **A** The poet loves sharks.
   - **B** Sharks are part of nature.
   - **C** Sharks are top predators.
3. Which photo suits Poem 2?

   A (1) **B** (2) **C** (3)
4. How are the poems similar?
   - **A** They both tell about ocean animals.
   - **B** They have the same subject.
   - **C** They tell you what to think about great white sharks.
5. Which adjective could belong in both poems?
   - **A** scary
   - **B** vicious
   - **C** impressive
6. Which poem best matches your opinion of sharks? Make sure you give reasons in your answer.

....

....

....

....

....

Now write!

Write a poem about an animal. Use describing words that tell readers what you think about the animal.

Note: The texts are imaginative—poems. They make use of evaluative language to present points of view. They use adjectives.

Answers and explanations on p. 86

Step-by-step guide to inferring questions

To answer **inferring** questions you need to use the clues in the text and read between the lines.

Use this **Step-by-step guide** to help you read the text and make **inferences** to answer the questions below. Circle the correct answers or write your answer on the lines.

STEP ①	**Skim** the texts. **Think**.	✪ **Skim** over the texts and the illustration. **Read** the title, *Wanted*. **Predict** what the texts might be about.
STEP ②	**Read** the texts. **Think**.	✪ **Re-read** the parts that you don't understand. **Think**. What do you know about the subject?

Wanted

Police need help to find a girl who broke into the house of three bears yesterday morning. When the bears got home from their walk they found that some porridge was missing, a chair was broken and a girl in dirty, old clothes was asleep in Baby's bed. The girl ran away when Mother Bear screamed.

Police say the girl later wrote a letter to Baby Bear. Police want to find the girl. They are worried about her.

Dear Little Bear

I am sorry. I couldn't help it. I had nowhere else to go. I am all alone.

From Goldilocks

Question 1 **Why did Mother Bear scream?**

A The porridge was missing.   B The girl ran away.   C There was a girl in Baby's bed.

STEP ③	**Read** the question. Work out what type of question it is.	✪ This is an **inferring** question. **Think** about what caused Mother Bear to scream.
STEP ④	Work out how to answer the question.	✪ Use clues in the text. **Scan** the text. Find the part about Mother Bear's scream. **Read** between the lines to **infer** why she screamed.

Answer: C is correct. You read *a girl ... was asleep in Baby's bed. The girl ran away when Mother Bear screamed (see lines 7–9)*. You can work out that Mother Bear screamed when she saw the girl in Baby's bed. It gave her a fright. **A** is incorrect because missing porridge would not make the mother scream. **B** is incorrect because the girl ran away after the mother screamed.

Question 2 **Why are police *worried* (line 11) about the girl?**

A She broke into the bears' house.
B She might steal more porridge.
C Her letter says she has nowhere else to go.

STEP 3	**Read** the question. Work out what type of question it is.	✪ This is an **inferring** question. **Think** about why the police were worried.
STEP 4	Work out how to answer the question.	✪ Use clues in the text. **Scan** the text to find clues about the police and the girl. **Read** between the lines.

Answer: C is correct. You read the letter from Goldilocks. Police would be worried that Goldilocks might have nowhere to live. **A** and **B** are incorrect because you can infer that the police are not worried about the porridge or that Goldilocks broke into the bears' house.

Question 3 **Why did Goldilocks eat the porridge?**

A She was in trouble.
B She was hungry.
C She was playing a trick on the bears.

STEP 3	Read the question. Work out what type of question it is.	✪ This is an **inferring** question. **Think** about why Goldilocks ate the porridge.
STEP 4	Work out how to answer the question.	✪ Use clues in the text. **Scan** the text. **Re-read** the parts that tell you about Goldilocks and the porridge. **Think**.

Answer: B is correct. You read *I am sorry. I couldn't help it (see line 14)*. You can work out that Goldilocks is sorry for all the things she did in the bears' house, including eating the porridge. You can work out that Goldilocks ate the porridge because she was hungry. **A** is incorrect. Goldilocks wasn't in trouble with the bears until after she ate the porridge. **C** is incorrect. You can work out that Goldilocks did not eat the porridge for fun.

Question 4 **The title of the text is *Wanted*. What did Goldilocks want?**

....

....

STEP 3	**Read** the question. Work out what type of question it is.	✪ This is an **inferring** question. **Think** about what Goldilocks wanted.
STEP 4	Work out how to answer the question.	✪ Use clues in the text. **Think**. **Read** between the lines.

Answer: Goldilocks wanted food and somewhere to go. Perhaps she also wanted to make friends with Baby Bear.

Now write!

Write what you predict will happen next.

Note: The texts are imaginative—a news item and a letter. They make use of the characters and setting from the folktale, *Goldilocks and the Three Bears*.

Inferring questions

Use the **Step-by-step guide** on pages 28–29 to help you read the text and make **inferences** to answer the questions below. Circle the correct answers or write your answer on the lines.

Peter has a feast

'Now, my dears,' said old Mrs. Rabbit one morning, 'You may go into the fields or down the lane, but don't go into Mr. McGregor's garden. Your father had an accident there; he was put in a pie by Mrs. McGregor.'

Flopsy, Mopsy and Cotton-tail who were good little bunnies went down the lane together to gather blackberries.

But Peter who was very naughty, ran straight away to Mr. McGregor's garden and squeezed under the gate!

First he ate some lettuces and some French beans and then he ate some radishes and then, feeling rather sick, he went to look for some parsley*.

*a herb that can help cure upset tummies

From *Peter Rabbit* by Beatrix Potter, 1902

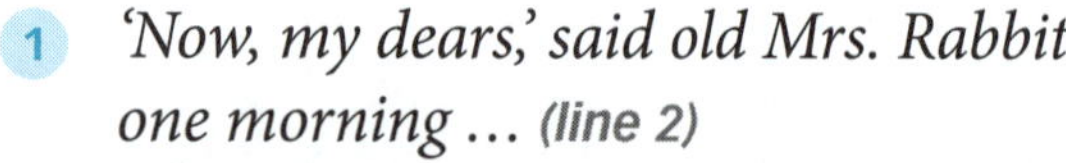

1. *'Now, my dears,' said old Mrs. Rabbit one morning …* (line 2)

   Mrs. Rabbit is talking to

   A her old friends.
   B her children.
   C her new neighbours.

2. What had happened to Mr. Rabbit?

   A He ran away from the family.
   B He was eaten.
   C He ate too much.

3. Mrs. Rabbit warns the rabbits not to go into Mr. McGregor's garden because

   A he will catch them and have them put in a pie.
   B they will get sick from eating his crops.
   C Mrs. McGregor will keep them for pets.

4. What causes Peter to feel sick?

   A He catches a germ.
   B He eats a worm.
   C He eats too much.

5. Why does Peter go to look for parsley?

   A He is a greedy rabbit.
   B It is his favourite herb.
   C He hopes it will stop him feeling sick.

6. Why does the author say Flopsy, Mopsy and Cotton-tail are *good little bunnies* (lines 6–7)?

   ....

   ....

   ....

Now write!

Write a story about someone getting into trouble.

Note: The text is imaginative—a narrative. The animal characters are given human qualities.

Answers and explanations on p. 87

Inferring questions

Use the **Step-by-step guide** on pages 28–29 to help you read the text and make **inferences** to answer the questions below. Circle the correct answers or write your answer on the lines.

Wally the wombat

Wally poked his hairy nose out from the huge burrow entrance. His tummy was grumbling. He sniffed the air. His nose told him which way to go.

The stars twinkled as he waddled out. He waddled past the sand mound he'd built with his strong claws. He waddled across the second runway to his burrow. He waddled past the trees alongside the dry creek bed. He sniffed as he waddled and he waddled on until he reached the native grass. He liked the black speargrass and the golden beard grass. He used his strong teeth to grind the leaves.

It was summertime, the time for bushfires. He was safe in his burrow but he knew the fires could burn all the grass.

He sensed it was nearly daylight; time to go home.

1 What time of day was it?
- A night-time
- B day time
- C lunch time

2 When does Wally eat?
- A in the morning
- B all day
- C in the night

3 Why do bushfires worry Wally?
- A They come in the summertime.
- B They destroy his food.
- C They burn his burrow.

4 Where does Wally sleep?
- A on the sand mound
- B in the grass
- C in a burrow

5 How does Wally find food?
- A He uses his strong claws.
- B He smells it.
- C He looks for it.

6 What does Wally eat?

....

....

Now write!

Write a story about an animal in the wild. Do some research first so you know how and where the animal lives, what it eats and what it does. Write what the animal might think about.

Notes: The text is imaginative—a narrative. It is written in the third person from an animal character's point of view. The animal is given human emotions and thoughts. The text shows how authors use factual research when creating imaginative texts. The text makes use of action (doing) verbs (*waddled*, *sniffed*).

Answers and explanations on p. 87

Inferring questions

Use the **Step-by-step guide** on pages 28–29 to help you read the text and make **inferences** to answer the questions below. Circle the correct answers or write your answers on the lines.

Big brother and little bother

My name is Ben. This is my little brother. →

His name is Charlie. He is only a baby. I am mostly glad I have a little brother but he can sometimes be a big bother.

Mum tells me to keep quiet when Charlie is sleeping. I find this is a bother.

Sometimes, when he cries loudly, I feel like this. →

I want Mum to make Charlie keep quiet. When I say this Mum gets bothered. She says to go in my room and chill out.

Charlie takes up a lot of Mum's time. I like being the big brother but a big brother sometimes wants his mum too. And little brothers can be big bothers even without trying.

1. *Mum tells me to keep quiet when Charlie is sleeping* (line 5).

   What does this mean?

   A Ben always makes too much noise.
   B Ben likes to wake the baby.
   C Mum doesn't want Ben to wake Charlie.

2. How does Ben feel when Charlie cries loudly?

   A worried **B** annoyed **C** sad

3. Why does Mum send Ben to his room?

   A She is angry that Charlie cries.
   B She is busy with Charlie.
   C She thinks Ben needs to calm down.

4. What does *even without trying* (line 12) tell you about Charlie?

   ....

   ....

5. *But a big brother sometimes wants his mum too* (line 11).

   What does this suggest?

   A Ben is a little jealous of the baby.
   B Ben needs help with homework.
   C Ben wants to be the baby again.

6. *I want Mum to make Charlie keep quiet. When I say this Mum gets bothered* (lines 8–9).

   Why does mum get bothered?

   ....

   ....

   ....

Now write!

Write a description of a family member. Include your opinions about things the person does.

Note: The text is informative—a description. It is written in the first person. It includes reported speech (*Mum says* ...).

Answers and explanations on pp. 87–88

Inferring questions

Use the **Step-by-step guide** on pages 28–29 to help you read the text and make **inferences** to answer the questions below. Circle the correct answers or write your answer on the lines.

Should there be a set bedtime for seven- and eight-year-olds?

Toby: I don't think children should have any set bedtime. It's healthier to go to sleep when you're tired.

Anh: But if it was left to me I'd stay up late then not wake up for school.

Hannah: I'm the same. I need a set bedtime. But I hate having it!

Jordan: I sleep through the alarm if I stay up late. My 'lights out' is at 8.30.

Hannah: Mine's 8.00.

Anh: So's mine. I have to get up at 6.30. Having a set bedtime is a real help.

Jordan: I don't like it when I'm watching something on TV and I have to stop because it's bedtime.

Hannah: Me neither. At least you should be allowed to bend the rules sometimes, don't you think?

Anh and Jordan: Yes!

1. Who agrees with Toby that children should not have a set bedtime?
   A Anh **B** no-one **C** Hannah

2. Who likes the idea of a set bedtime?
   A Anh
   B Jordan
   C no-one

3. Which idea is popular with the children?
   A Have a set bedtime but bend the rules sometimes.
   B Have a set bedtime and don't bend the rules.
   C Don't have a set bedtime.

4. The main reason the children approve of a set bedtime is that it means
   A they wake up in time for school in the morning.
   B they are able to sleep in.
   C they know they need 10 hours sleep to stay healthy.

5. How do Hannah's and Jordan's opinions differ?
   A Hannah likes the idea of a set bedtime more than Jordan.
   B Hannah likes the idea of a set bedtime less than Jordan.
   C They have exactly the same feelings about bedtime.

6. Why doesn't Toby call out *Yes* with the other children?

   ....

   ....

Now write!

Do you think children your age should have a set bedtime? Give reasons for your opinion.

Note: The text is persuasive—a discussion. The children give their points of view about a topic.

Answers and explanations on p. 88

Inferring questions

Use the **Step-by-step guide** on pages 28–29 to help you read the text and make **inferences** to answer the questions below. Circle the correct answers or write your answer on the lines.

The trumpet player

There was a knock on the classroom door.

'Ms Brown would like to hear Amy play her trumpet now,' said the messenger.

'Amy, are you ready? Off you go,' said Ms Scott.

My heart did a somersault. This was my chance.

I went to get my trumpet from my locker. I hardly noticed Evie tapping my arm or Susie pretending to trip me.

When I arrived in the music room, Ms Brown asked me to play the piece I'd been practising. I took a deep breath and began.

....

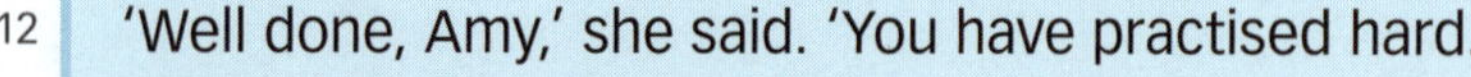

'Well done, Amy,' she said. 'You have practised hard.'

'Yes, Ms Brown,' I said.

'I think we can enter you in the eisteddfod. What do you think of that?'

'Oh yes, please, Ms Brown,' I replied. My dream had come true.

1. Amy's heart does a somersault because she feels
   - **A** nervous and excited.
   - **B** calm and fearful.
   - **C** surprised and unhappy.

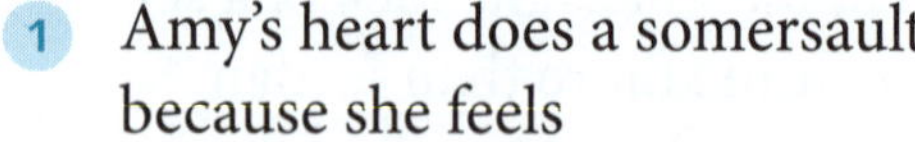

2. Why does Amy hardly notice what Susie and Evie do to her?
   - **A** She needs new glasses.
   - **B** They are just being friendly.
   - **C** She is thinking about playing her trumpet.
3. Who are Susie and Evie?
   - **A** teachers who help Ms Scott
   - **B** Amy's sisters
   - **C** children in Amy's class
4. Why does Amy take a deep breath?
   - **A** She feels dizzy.
   - **B** She needs air to blow into her trumpet.
   - **C** It is a bad habit she can't stop.
5. *'You have practised hard.'* **(line 12)**

   Ms Brown's words suggest Amy's trumpet playing
   - **A** has improved a great deal.
   - **B** needs a lot more improvement.
   - **C** won't ever improve again.
6. What was Amy's dream?

   ....

   ....

Now write!

Write a story about a character who has a dream. What is the dream? How does the character feel? What happens?

Note: The text is imaginative—a narrative. It uses conversation and tells about events that build to a climax.

Answers and explanations on p. 88

Inferring questions

Use the **Step-by-step guide** on pages 28–29 to help you read the text and make **inferences** to answer the questions below. Circle the correct answers or write your answers on the lines.

Whose house is it anyway?

There's a giant in our house
and I find it very scary.
I'm just a tiny mouse but
He's metres tall and hairy!
He likes to yell, 'It's ready!'
I don't know what that means.
But then more giants come running,
Not so tall—more in-betweens.
I hear them chomping, chomping,
And I say to Mr Mouse,
'Please, dear, I think it's time we left.
We need another house.'

1. What is the *giant*?
   - **A** a man
   - **B** a very tall mouse
   - **C** a talking mouse

2. Why does the mouse think the giant is scary?
   - **A** It has large teeth.
   - **B** It's much bigger than the mouse.
   - **C** The mouse is shy.

3. Why does the giant yell '*It's ready!*' *(line 6)*?
   - **A** He has set the mouse trap.
   - **B** It's time for a bath.
   - **C** The food is ready to eat.

4. Who are the *in-betweens* *(line 9)*?
   - **A** small giants
   - **B** other humans
   - **C** teenagers

5. Why are they *chomping, chomping* *(line 10)*?

   ....

   ....

6. Why does Mrs Mouse want another house?

   ....

   ....

Now write!

Write a poem about something that you find scary.

Note: The text is imaginative—a poem. It is written from an animal character's point of view. The animal characters are given human qualities.

Answers and explanations on pp. 88–89

Inferring questions

Use the **Step-by-step guide** on pages 28–29 to help you read the text and make **inferences** to answer the questions below. Circle the correct answers or write your answer on the lines.

Mia's mistake

'Hey!' yelled Mia. 'That's my bag.' Mia jumped up.

On the other side of the park a boy she didn't know had picked up her school bag. He was walking away with it. Not again, thought Mia. Please, no. I can't lose another one.

'Hey!' Mia yelled loudly. The boy didn't seem to hear her. He crossed the street.

Mia was starting to panic. Everyone at the park was looking at Mia; everyone except the boy who had stolen her school bag. Mia was going to be in trouble when her mother arrived. She needed to catch the boy and get it back. But she wasn't allowed to leave the park. Not after last time. She had to be there when Mum arrived at 4 o'clock. Mum hated being late for work at the restaurant. But Mia had to get her bag back.

She started to run.

1. *Not again, thought Mia* (line 4). What does this imply?
   - **A** The boy had taken Mia's school bag before.
   - **B** The boy had crossed the street before.
   - **C** Mia had lost her school bag before.

2. Mia's attitude suggests she is trying to
   - **A** start a fight.
   - **B** make friends with the boy.
   - **C** avoid getting into trouble from her mum.

3. Why wasn't Mia allowed to leave the park?
   - **A** If she's not at the park it makes her mum late for work.
   - **B** Her mum worries that Mia might get lost.
   - **C** Mia might get run over by a car.

4. What does Mia do when the boy doesn't hear her?
   - **A** She runs back into the park to wait for her mum.
   - **B** She yells very loudly at the boy.
   - **C** She chases the boy.

5. When did the events occur?
   - **A** before school
   - **B** after school
   - **C** on the weekend

6. Why might the text be called *Mia's mistake*?

   ....

   ....

   ....

Now write!

Write a story about a problem faced by a character.

Or write what happens next in the story *Mia's mistake*.

Note: The text is imaginative—a narrative. It is written in the third person and gives the main character's point of view. It includes quoted speech.

Answers and explanations on p. 89

Inferring questions

Use the **Step-by-step guide** on pages 28–29 to help you read the text and make **inferences** to answer the questions below. Circle the correct answers or write your answers on the lines.

The invitation

Text 1

Dear girl with the red hood

I am a nice wolf. Do not believe what people say about me. Yes, I have sharp teeth but I won't bite you. (Girls in red hoods are not my favourite food.) Yes, I have big ears but that's so I can listen to the birds sing. Yes, I have a long nose but that's so I can smell the roses. Yes, I have sharp claws but that's so I can comb my fur.

Want to be my friend? We can play hide-and-seek. We can sing with the birds and pick roses. I will show you my den. Come for dinner.

Best wishes

Wolfie

Text 2

Dear Reader

What would you do if a wolf invited you for dinner? Would you trust him? The girl with the red hood believed the wolf. She went to his den and he had her for dinner. The moral of the story is 'Never trust a wolf'.

Kind regards

The narrator

1 What have people said about Wolfie?

- A that he's handsome
- B that girls in red hoods are his favourite food
- C that he's dangerous

2 *Girls in red hoods are not my favourite food* (lines 6–7).

Why does Wolfie say this?

- A to make the girl think she won't be eaten
- B to make the girl think she will be eaten
- C to frighten the girl

3 *Come for dinner* (line 13).

What does this suggest?

- A The wolf is a tricky character.
- B The wolf is proud of his home.
- C The wolf likes to cook.

4 What happened when the girl went to the wolf's den?

- A The girl and the wolf ate dinner together.
- B The wolf cooked dinner.
- C The wolf ate the girl.

5 *The girl … believed the wolf* (lines 20–21).

What did the girl believe?

....

....

6 Why should you '*Never trust a wolf*' (line 23)?

....

....

Now write!

Imagine you are a story character. Write a letter to another story character. Give your point of view.

Note: The texts are imaginative—letters. The characters are from the fairytale *Red Riding Hood*. The narrator speaks to the reader in Text 2 (*Dear Reader …*).

Answers and explanations on p. 89

Step-by-step guide to language questions

To answer **language** questions you need to think about the way language is used in the text.

Use this **Step-by-step guide** to help you read the text and examine the way **language** is used to answer the questions below. Circle the correct answers or write your answer on the lines.

STEP 1	**Skim** the text. **Think**.	✪ **Skim** over the text. Look at how it is set out. Notice that it is in paragraphs. **Think** about what the illustration shows you. **Read** the title, *Clouds*. **Predict** what the text might be about.
STEP 2	**Read** the text. **Think**. Does the text make sense to you?	✪ **Re-read** any parts that you don't understand. ✪ **Think**. What do you know about the subject?

Clouds

What are clouds? Clouds are masses of water vapour.

All air contains water vapour. As the sun heats the air, the air rises. When the air rises to a certain height, it then cools. The water vapour in this cooler air forms into tiny droplets of water or ice crystals. When these droplets mass together they form a cloud.

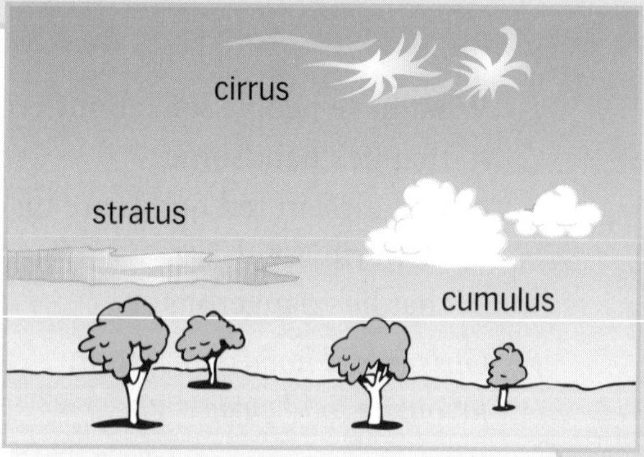

Three types of clouds

Cirrus clouds are thin and wispy. They look like streamers wafting across the sky. Stratus clouds are greyish in colour. They look like fog that hasn't come down to ground level. Cumulus clouds are puffy and look like floating cotton wool.

Question 1 What do the words *cirrus*, *stratus* and *cumulus* name?

A droplets of air   B types of clouds   C forms of water

STEP 3	**Read** the question. Work out what type of question it is.	✪ This is a **language** terminology question. **Think** about what the words cirrus, stratus and cumulus name.
STEP 4	Work out how to answer the question.	✪ **Re-read** the parts of the text where these words are used. Work out what the words name.

Answer: B is correct. The words *cirrus*, *stratus* and *cumulus* name different types of clouds. **A** and **C** are incorrect as cirrus, stratus and cumulus are not names of droplets of air or forms of water.

Question 2 The language of the text is mainly

A factual. B exaggerated. C humorous.

STEP 3	**Read** the question. Work out what type of question it is.	This is a **language** question. **Think** about what kind of language is used in the text.
STEP 4	Work out how to answer the question.	**Re-read** the text to decide whether the language is mainly factual, exaggerated or amusing.

Answer: A is correct. The language is mainly factual. The text gives information about what clouds are and what they look like. **B** and **C** are incorrect. None of the language is exaggerated or humorous.

Question 3 Comparing cirrus clouds to streamers tells you that they are

A long and thin. B fat and round. C dense and heavy.

STEP 3	**Read** the question. Work out what type of question it is.	This is a **language** question. **Think** about why the clouds are compared to streamers.
STEP 4	Work out how to answer the question.	**Re-read** the part where cirrus clouds are described. **Think** about what the description tells you about cirrus clouds.

Answer: A is correct. You read that *cirrus clouds are thin and wispy. They look like streamers wafting across the sky (see line 10).* The comparison with streamers suggests that cirrus clouds look long and thin. **B** and **C** are incorrect. The comparison with streamers does not suggest that cirrus clouds are fat and round, or dense and heavy.

Question 4 Why does the writer compare cumulus clouds with cotton wool?

....

....

STEP 3	**Read** the question. Work out what type of question it is.	This is a **language** question. **Think** about why cumulus clouds are compared to cotton wool.
STEP 4	Work out how to answer the question.	**Re-read** the part of the text where cumulus clouds are described. **Think** about what the words cotton wool tell you about the clouds.

Answer: The writer compares cumulus clouds to cotton wool to show what the clouds look like. They are white, they look soft and fluffy, and they appear rounded in shape like balls of cotton wool in the sky.

Now write!

Write an explanation for something else in nature. For example, what is rain, fog or hail?

Note: The text is informative—an explanation. It uses technical terms and descriptive language. It uses the subordinating conjunction *when* to link clauses in a time sequence.

Language questions

Use the **Step-by-step guide** on pages 38–39 to help you read the text and examine the way **language** is used to answer the questions below. Circle the correct answers or write your answer on the lines.

Moving house

Boxes here.
Boxes there.
Boxes—you guessed—
Everywhere.

I've packed my bat.
I've packed my skates.
My racquet's in. Oh!
I'll miss my mates.

I'll miss my tree
in the park next door.
'No worries,' says Mum.
'You'll find plenty more.'

The new place has
a garage wall.
I can practise there
with my soccer ball.

School's not far.
I'll walk each day.
That's if we *ever*
get away.

Boxes here.
Boxes there.
Boxes—you guessed—
Everywhere.

by Gretchen

1 *My racquet's in (line 8).*

Where is Gretchen's racquet?

A in the house
B in the boxes
C in the way

2 Gretchen says *Oh! (line 8)* because she suddenly

A feels frightened.
B feels happy.
C realises she's leaving her mates.

3 Mum uses the expression *No worries (line 12)* to mean

A 'I've got enough worries. Don't add to them.'
B 'You'll be right.'
C 'Don't blame me.'

4 Which line addresses the reader?

A Boxes—you guessed—
B I'll miss my mates
C My racket's in. Oh!

5 The word *ever (line 20)* is in italics to show

A how long a time moving house is taking.
B how quickly moving house happens.
C that Gretchen doesn't want to move house.

6 Why is stanza one repeated at the end of the poem?

....

....

....

Now write!

Write a poem about a change in your life.

Note: The text is imaginative—a poem. It has six stanzas and uses rhyme. The first stanza is repeated at the end.

Answers and explanations on p. 90

Language questions

Use the **Step-by-step guide** on pages 38–39 to help you read the text and examine the way **language** is used to answer the questions below. Circle the correct answers or write your answer on the lines.

Apricot balls

This recipe is good for snacks. It is also a healthy lunch-box treat.

Ingredients

1 cup dried apricots, finely chopped

½ cup desiccated coconut

½ cup chopped unsalted cashews or almonds

2 tablespoons coconut oil

1 tablespoon honey

extra desiccated coconut for rolling

Method

Mix all ingredients.

Roll into small balls.

Roll balls in extra coconut.

Store in fridge.

Not suitable for people with allergies to nuts.

Not suitable for people who are allergic to sulphite preservatives in dried fruit.

1 Why does the recipe use *also* in *It is also a healthy lunch-box treat* (lines 2–3)?

A It's tasty and healthy.

B It's a treat as a snack bar.

C It's good as a snack and with lunch.

2 What does *Not suitable* (line 19) mean in the text?

A not useful

B not tasty

C not to be eaten

3 This food will taste

A sour.

B sweet.

C salty.

4 Another word for *Store* (line 16) in the text is

A buy. **B** keep. **C** eat.

5 The *Method* (line 12) tells you

A what steps to follow.

B which ingredients to use.

C what amounts to use.

6 Which two words in the text mean that moisture has been taken out?

....

....

Now write!

Describe a lunch-box treat that you recommend.

Note: The text is informative—a recipe. It is written in logical order. It uses commands and technical terminology.

Answers and explanations on p. 90

Language questions

Use the **Step-by-step guide** on pages 38–39 to help you read the text and examine the way **language** is used to answer the questions below. Circle the correct answers or write your answer on the lines.

New | Reply | Delete | Archive | Junk | Sweep

Litter report

Hi Nana

Guess what! I reported a litterer. Dad was the reporter, really, because you have to be 18. But I helped. I took the photo. We saw someone toss a cigarette butt out of a car window and Dad said, 'Quick! Take a photo of the car. Make sure you get the number plate.' So I did. Then we filled in an online report and attached the photo. The car owner will get fined. Dad says the fine could be $220.

Dad said it is our duty to report litterers because litter hurts animals. Litter traps animals or chokes them. They eat it and it poisons them. Also, cigarette butts cause fires.

I am now always on the lookout for litterers.

Miss you, love CJ

1. *Guess what!* (line 4). What does this exclamation tell Nana?
   - A CJ is excited.
   - B CJ is asking Nana to guess what happened.
   - C CJ is talking to Nana on the phone.
2. *We saw someone …* (line 5). Who is *we*?
   - A Nana and CJ
   - B Dad and CJ
   - C CJ
3. What word in the text is used to mean 'wrongdoer'?
   - A owner
   - B reporter
   - C litterer
4. What does *duty* (line 9) mean?
   - A business
   - B responsibility
   - C purpose
5. How does CJ keep a lookout for litterers?
   - A with binoculars
   - B with a camera
   - C with his or her eyes
6. *So I did* (line 7).

   What did CJ do?

   ....

   ....

Now write!

Think about an issue in your local area. It might be littering, recycling, the local playgrounds or any other topic. Write your opinions in an email to a friend or family member.

Note: The text is informative—an email. It shares a personal response and recounts an event. It deals with the idea of being a responsible citizen.

Answers and explanations on p. 90

Language questions

Use the **Step-by-step guide** on pages 38–39 to help you read the text and examine the way **language** is used to answer the questions below. Circle the correct answers or write your answer on the lines.

At the museum

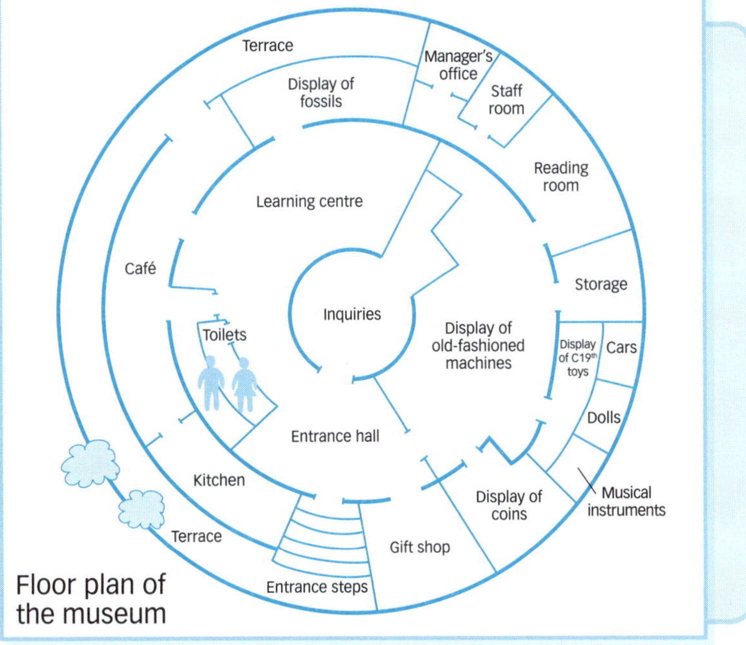

Floor plan of the museum

1 Where would you go for information about the museum?
 A Staff room
 B Learning centre
 C Inquiries

2 Dolls are ________________ Musical instruments and Cars.
 A above
 B between
 C underneath

3 Where would objects be kept when not on display?
 A Storage
 B Kitchen
 C Reading room

4 Which room is an office for the person in charge of the Museum?
 A Gift shop
 B Manager's office
 C Staff room

5 To get to the Learning centre from the Entrance hall you would turn
 A left and go past the toilets.
 B right and go through the C19th toy display.
 C around and walk out onto the Terrace.

6 In which room would you find the skull of an ancient diprotodon? Explain how you know.

....

....

....

....

Now write!

Draw a floor plan of the inside of your home. Label the rooms. Mark the doors and windows.

Note: The text is informative—a map.

Answers and explanations on pp. 90–91

Language questions

Use the **Step-by-step guide** on pages 38–39 to help you read the text and examine the way **language** is used to answer the questions below. Circle the correct answers or write your answer on the lines.

Things to do when I'm bored

1 Make a sock puppet and use it to tell Billy, my little brother, a story.
2 Use sheets, brooms and cardboard cartons to make a cubby house.
3 Find and observe a bug in the garden, then sketch it.
4 Make some paper aeroplanes to fly with my friend, Ichiro.
5 Log on to the library's website and borrow an eBook.
6 Make a diorama of the seaside.
7 Volunteer to wash my Nan's car.
8 Collect something, e.g. coins, stamps or riddles.
9 Practise taking better photographs.
10 Plant a vegetable garden (not broccoli).
11 Start a new hobby (perhaps cooking or maybe astronomy).
12 Hide a 'treasure' and make up clues for a treasure hunt.

by Alex

1 Personal details about Alex's friends and family are included in

- **A** 1 and 4.
- **B** 2 and 6.
- **C** 11 and 12.

2 The odd one out in the things Alex thinks of collecting is

A coins. **B** stamps. **C** riddles.

3 *Plant a vegetable garden (not broccoli)* (line 11).

The brackets are used to suggest that broccoli is

- **A** a vegetable that Alex doesn't want in the garden.
- **B** a vegetable that Alex wants in the garden.
- **C** not a vegetable.

4 Which items show that Alex thinks of other people's needs?

- **A** 6 and 9
- **B** 1 and 7
- **C** 5 and 12

5 The brackets used in number 11 show Alex has not yet decided

- **A** if astronomy is a good idea for a hobby.
- **B** which hobby would be the better choice.
- **C** if having a hobby is a good idea.

6 Which activity on Alex's list most interests you? Why?

....

....

Now write!

Write a list of things you could do if you were feeling bored.

Note: The text is informative—a list that shares a personal response.

Answers and explanations on p. 91

Language questions

Use the **Step-by-step guide** on pages 38–39 to help you read the text and examine the way **language** is used to answer the questions below. Circle the correct answers or write your answer on the lines.

Disappointment

Dad: Cheer up. You did your best. That's what counts.
Ava: I know, but I wanted to do better than that.
Dad: Did you have fun?
Ava: Yes, of course. I always have fun at Little Athletics.
Dad: Well then, why are you complaining?
Ava: I already told you. I should have done better.
Dad: Ava, tell me why you like to go each week.
Ava: Because it's fun.
Dad: Well it doesn't look like you're having fun now.
Ava: No.
Dad: Don't lose sight of why you go. You go to have fun first and foremost. You should be proud of yourself. I'm proud of you. You did really well. You're improving all the time.
Ava: I wish I'd trained harder.
Dad: Too late now. It's no use crying over spilt milk.

1 *I know, but I wanted to do better than that* (line 3).

What does Ava mean by *I know*?

A I know you are proud of me.
B I know I can do better.
C I know doing my best is what counts.

2 What does *counts* mean in *That's what counts* (line 2)?

A equals success
B adds up
C matters

3 *Don't lose sight …* (line 12)

What does this mean?

A Don't forget what's important.
B Don't go blind.
C Don't worry so much.

4 *It's no use crying over spilt milk* (line 15).

What does this mean?

A If you spill milk don't cry about it.
B There's no point being upset about something you can't change.
C Don't cry about things that upset you.

5 What does *foremost* (line 12) mean in the text?

A basically
B most importantly
C lastly

6 Why is the title *Disappointment*?

....

....

Now write!

Choose a scene from a story that involves two characters having a conversation. Write their conversation as a playscript.

Note: The text is imaginative—a conversation. The characters express feelings and emotions. The text uses colloquial language and idiomatic expressions (*It's no use crying over spilt milk.*).

Answers and explanations on p. 91

Language questions

Use the **Step-by-step guide** on pages 38–39 to help you read the text and examine the way **language** is used to answer the questions below. Circle the correct answers or write your answers on the lines.

The hare and the tortoise

Narrator: The hare and the tortoise had a race. This is what they said before the race.

Hare: (*hopping on the spot*) I am faster than that tortoise. I can run so fast that I'll be able to stop and have a nap along the way. I will beat that slow tortoise. I will win!

Tortoise: (*standing as still as a statue*) I will walk at a steady pace. I will keep walking until I finish the race. I will do my very best.

Narrator: The hare ran fast for a while, then had a nap beside the path. The tortoise plodded on and won the race. This is what they said after the race.

Hare: That tortoise must have cheated while I was asleep.

Tortoise: Slow and steady wins the race.

1. What does *steady* *(line 10)* mean?

   A even   B slow   C plodding

2. The writer uses the exclamation *I will win!* *(line 4)* to show that

   A the hare is angry.

   B the hare is surprised.

   C the hare is determined.

3. Which adjective describes the tortoise before the race?

   A excited   B calm   C boastful

4. Which adjective describes the hare before the race?

   A energetic   B sleepy   C foolish

5. Write a thought bubble for the tortoise during the race.

   ....

   ....

   ....

   ....

6. *Slow and steady wins the race* *(line 10)*.

   What does this mean?

   ....

   ....

   ....

   ....

   ....

Now write!

Choose a fable or tale. It might be an Aesop fable or a tale from any other origin. Rewrite it as a playscript. Use a narrator to tell the parts that the characters don't speak.

Note: The text is imaginative—a playscript. It is based on an Aesop fable, 'The hare and the tortoise.'

Answers and explanations on pp. 91–92

Language questions

Use the **Step-by-step guide** on pages 38–39 to help you read the text and examine the way **language** is used to answer the questions below. Circle the correct answers or write your answers on the lines.

Grandad

My grandad knows a lot of jokes. He makes me laugh. He even has a fart cushion. But he's not allowed to bring it to the dinner table. Dad says that would be inappropriate.

Grandad has bristly white eyebrows and a moustache. There's not much hair on his head but plenty growing out of his ears; Grandad the walrus.

He taught me how to play a word game called Scrabble. He used to always win but I started to beat him so now he cheats. He makes up words and he steals letters. I have to watch him like a hawk. He can be very tricky.

He rides a motor scooter to the shops. When he offers me a ride he says, 'M'lady, your chariot awaits.' It gives me the giggles.

1. What does *inappropriate* (line 5) mean?
   - **A** unacceptable
   - **B** suitable
   - **C** funny
2. What do Grandad's eyebrows feel like?
   - **A** soft
   - **B** prickly
   - **C** white
3. *I have to watch him like a hawk* (line 11). What does this mean?
   - **A** watch him with beady eyes
   - **B** watch him from up in the air
   - **C** watch him very carefully
4. Who wrote the text?
   - **A** the grandson
   - **B** the granddaughter
   - **C** Grandad
5. What is another name for *motor scooter* (line 12) used in the text?

   ....

6. *Grandad the walrus* (line 8). What does this mean?

   ....

   ....

   ....

   ....

Now write!

Write a description of someone you know. Try to usc language that helps others imagine exactly what the person is like.

Note: The text is informative—a description. It uses colloquial language and idiom, as well as simile, metaphor and quoted speech.

Answers and explanations on p. 92

Step-by-step guide to judgement questions

To answer **judgement** questions you need to think critically.

Use this **Step-by**-step guide to help you read the text and make **judgements** to answer the questions below. Circle the correct answers or write your answers on the lines.

STEP		
STEP ①	**Skim** the text. **Think**.	**Skim** over the text. Look at how it is set out. Notice that it is in paragraphs. **Think** about what the illustration shows you. **Read** the title, *Allergy trouble*. **Predict** what the text might be about.
STEP ②	**Read** the text. **Think**. Does the text make sense to you?	**Re-read** the parts that you don't understand. **Think**. What do you know about the subject?

Allergy trouble

My friend, Scarlet, is allergic to peanuts and tree nuts. They make her so sick she can't even breathe. She carries an EpiPen everywhere.

One day when Scarlet first visited my house she got sick. Mum had to call an ambulance. We worked out that my cousin had eaten peanut butter and then played with my toys. Mum thinks some traces of peanut butter must have been on the toys. When Scarlet touched them she got sick very quickly.

We never have tree nuts or peanut butter at my house any more so that Scarlet will be safe.

by Kate

Question 1 Does Kate care that there's no peanut butter at her house?

A Yes. She misses it.

B No. She likes Scarlet more than she likes peanut butter.

C Yes. She's annoyed that they can't have it anymore.

STEP		
STEP ③	**Read** the question. Work out what type of question it is.	This is a **judgement** question. **Think** about what Kate says about peanut butter in the text.
STEP ④	Work out how to answer the question.	**Re-read** the text if necessary. **Think** for yourself. Make a **judgement**.

Answer: B is correct. You should judge by the way Kate describes Scarlet's problem that she doesn't mind being without peanut butter. **A** and **C** are incorrect. You cannot judge that Kate misses peanut butter or is annoyed that she can't have it.

Question 2 Which statement best describes Kate and Scarlet.

A They are very good friends. B They are cousins. C They are friendly.

STEP 3	**Read** the question. Work out what type of question it is.	✪ This is a **judgement** question. **Think** about the way Kate talks about Scarlet in the text.
STEP 4	Work out how to answer the question.	✪ **Re-read** the text if necessary. **Think** for yourself. Make a **judgement**.

Answer: A is correct. You should judge by the way Kate tells you about Scarlet, and from the happy photo, that the two girls are very good friends. **B** and **C** are incorrect. You should judge that the girls are more than just friendly and that they are not cousins.

Question 3 Which statement is most likely to be true?

A Kate was excited about calling an ambulance.

B Kate was worried when Scarlet went in the ambulance.

C Kate is jealous of Scarlet because she went in an ambulance.

STEP 3	**Read** the question. Work out what type of question it is.	✪ This is a **judgement** question. **Think** about the things Kate says in the text.
STEP 4	Work out how to answer the question.	✪ **Re-read** the text if necessary. **Think** for yourself. Make a **judgement**.

Answer: B is correct. You can judge by the things Kate tells you about Scarlet's problem that she was worried about Scarlet. **A** and **C** are incorrect. You should judge that Scarlet was not excited about the ambulance or jealous that she did not go in it.

Question 4 How serious is Scarlet's allergy? Explain.

....

....

Answer: You should judge Scarlet's allergy to be very serious. You read that she gets so sick that *she can't even breathe (see line 3).* You read that Kate's mother *had to call an ambulance (see line 6)* and that Kate never has peanuts or tree nuts at home *so that Scarlet will be safe (see lines 11–12).*

Now write!

Would you like Kate as a friend? Explain. Or ask friends and classmates if they have allergies or know people with allergies. List the allergies and what problems they cause.

....

....

Note: The text is informative—a recount. It tells about events that took place.

Judgement questions

Use the **Step-by-step guide** on pages 48–49 to help you read the text and make **judgements** to answer the questions below. Circle the correct answers or write your answers on the lines.

Nicki's problem

It was going to be Nicki's mother's birthday tomorrow. Nicki wanted to buy her mother a birthday gift but she had no money. Last week she had $20. She had saved her pocket money and earned extra money doing jobs around the house. Now that was gone. She had spent all her money last weekend when she'd stayed at her dad's place. Her stepsister Rachel had lots of money. Rachel's mother had taken the girls to the shopping centre. Rachel had bought a lot of stuff and Nicki wanted to buy things too. And now Nicki would not be able to buy her mother a birthday gift. What could she do? She had until tomorrow morning to think of a solution.

1 Which do you think is true about Nicki?
- A She is selfish and only thinks of herself.
- B She is jealous of Rachel.
- C She made a mistake but plans to fix it.

2 What is Nicki's main feeling?
- A cheerfulness
- B anger
- C sadness

3 If Nicki could go back in time what would she do?
- A not spend all her money
- B not stay at her dad's
- C not go to the shopping centre with Rachel and her mum

4 Which statement is least likely to be true?
- A Rachel's mum is mean to Nicki.
- B Nicki and Rachel have fun together.
- C Nicki's dad likes Nicki staying over.

5 What might Nicki's mum think of Nicki's problem?

....

....

6 If you were Nicki what would you do? Explain.

....

....

....

Now write!

Write what Nicki does to solve her problem. Write in the third person.

Note: The text is imaginative—a narrative. It is written in the third person to give the point of view of the main character. It provides an orientation and a complication.

Answers and explanations on pp. 92–93

Judgement questions

Use the **Step-by-step guide** on pages 48–49 to help you read the text and make **judgements** to answer the questions below. Circle the correct answers or write your answers on the lines.

World Ranger Day

31 July is World Ranger Day. This special day makes people think about the important jobs that rangers do. Rangers protect the environment. In some countries a ranger's job is dangerous.

My mum is a ranger. She helps protect our Sea Country*. One of her jobs is to help sea turtles. She counts hatchlings and then makes sure the hatchlings get to the water. Last nesting season Mum was excited because she got to watch a female lay her eggs, then crawl back into the sea. After the female left, Mum and other rangers had to move the eggs higher up the beach so they wouldn't drown when they hatched. Last month Mum helped build a fence to keep four-wheel-drive vehicles off the beach where the turtles nest.

I want to be a ranger when I grow up.

by Cathy

*Sea Country refers to areas of Australia's coast managed by Indigenous people.

1 Cathy thinks a ranger's job is
- A boring.
- B hard work.
- C important.

2 How does Cathy feel about her mum?
- A worried
- B inspired
- C jealous

3 How does Cathy want you to feel about sea turtles?
- A worried for their future
- B that they are in safe hands
- C excited that they lay eggs

4 What does Cathy think about Sea Country?
- A protective and proud
- B not very interested
- C doesn't care

5 Why do you think sea turtles need rangers' help?

....

....

6 Does the text make you want to be a ranger? Explain.

....

....

....

Now write!

Write what you would like to be or do when you grow up. Include information about people who have influenced you and why.

Note: The text is informative—a personal response.

Answers and explanations on p. 93

Judgement questions

Use the **Step-by-step guide** on pages 48–49 to help you read the text and make **judgements** to answer the questions below. Circle the correct answers or write your answers on the lines.

Pets

Harry

Vivienne has a dog called Harry that she walks every day. Sometimes she takes Harry to the dog park where he loves to run off leash with his friends from the neighbourhood. Harry sleeps on his bed in the laundry.

Vivienne has jobs to do for Harry. She feeds Harry, brushes him, collects his poo and gives him plenty of fresh water. Vivienne's mother helps when Harry needs a bath. Harry tries to escape at bath time.

Molly

Will has a cat called Molly. Molly sits on Will's lap while he does his homework. She sleeps at the end of Will's bed. Sometimes Molly likes attention. Sometimes she prefers to be left in peace. Will has learned to read her signals. He says she is very smart and also a greedy guts.

1 Make a judgement about Vivienne.

- **A** She adores Harry but complains about her jobs.
- **B** She is a responsible pet owner.
- **C** She sometimes tries to get out of her jobs.

2 Which description best fits Harry?

- **A** a sociable and energetic dog
- **B** a great guard dog
- **C** a clean but lazy dog

3 What is Harry thinking in the photo?

- **A** Take me home. I'm tired.
- **B** Will I need a bath after this?
- **C** Let's run faster.

4 What is Molly thinking in the photo?

- **A** I wish Will understood me better.
- **B** Will made a mistake in his homework today.
- **C** Will is a very obedient human.

5 Which pet would better suit an elderly person in a home unit? Explain.

....

....

6 Which pet would you prefer? Why?

....

....

Now write!

What is your favourite kind of pet? Why?

Note: The texts are informative—descriptions.

Answers and explanations on p. 93

Judgement questions

Use the **Step-by-step guide** on pages 48–49 to help you read the text and make **judgements** to answer the questions below. Circle the correct answers or write your answer on the lines.

Chinese New Year

Dad, Chen has invited me to Chinese New Year with her family.

That's a very nice invitation, Mary Jo. Would you like to go?

I would. But …

Yes?

Well, I hope I'll know what to do.

Chen will help you.

Later that night …

It was amazing, Dad. There were all Chen's relatives around a huge table at the restaurant. Chen taught me how to use chopsticks.

Did you see the parade?

We did. There was a Chinese dragon puppet. There were firecrackers to frighten the bad spirits away. Chen and I got a red envelope with 'lucky money'. I had the best time.

1. Mary Jo's father thinks
   - A Mary Jo must accept Chen's invitation.
   - B Mary Jo should decide if she wants to accept the invitation.
   - C It would be better if Mary Jo stayed at home.
2. Mary Jo is worried because
   - A she is unsure about how to follow Chinese customs.
   - B she doesn't know how to reply politely to the invitation.
   - C she doesn't want to accept the invitation.
3. How does Chen feel about her Chinese background?
   - A proud B worried C curious
4. Mary Jo's relationship with her father is
   - A unhappy.
   - B unfriendly.
   - C trusting.
5. How did Mary Jo feel at the end of the night?
   - A frightened and worried
   - B jealous and annoyed
   - C excited and happy
6. What did Mary Jo learn about herself from this new experience?

   ....

   ....

   ....

Now write!

Write about a celebration you have enjoyed.

Note: The text is informative—a personal conversation. It uses questions and answers.

Answers and explanations on p. 94

Judgement questions

Use the **Step-by-step guide** on pages 48–49 to help you read the text and make **judgements** to answer the questions below. Circle the correct answers or write your answer on the lines.

A Dreaming story: Tiddalik

Tiddalik, the giant frog, was very thirsty. He drank all the water in the billabong. He hopped to the river and drank until the river was dry. Soon he'd drunk all the water in the land. He could barely move.

This was an emergency for the other animals. They would have to get the water back somehow. The wombat said they should try to make Tiddalik laugh. So they did funny dances in front of him. He didn't even smile.

The eel felt so angry with Tiddalik that his body twisted and turned with fury. That made Tiddalik laugh! He couldn't stop. The water poured from his mouth. He shrank to his present size. And soon, thank goodness, the waterholes were full once again. Tiddalik crept away to hide, forever after, in the reeds and the mud.

1. Tiddalik is
   - **A** thoughtful and friendly.
   - **B** greedy and selfish.
   - **C** mean and ugly.
2. What caused an emergency for the other animals?
   - **A** They had to find a way to help Tiddalik move.
   - **B** They would die without water.
   - **C** They didn't have a plan.
3. Tiddalik didn't laugh at the animal's funny dances because
   - **A** his eyes were shut.
   - **B** he didn't think they were funny.
   - **C** he didn't want to lose any of the water he'd swallowed.
4. The eel
   - **A** had a better plan than the other animals.
   - **B** had never felt so angry before.
   - **C** didn't know his actions would solve the emergency.
5. Why does Tiddalik hide in the reeds and the mud?
   - **A** He thinks he'll find some more water there.
   - **B** He feels bad about his behaviour.
   - **C** That is where he lives.
6. What is the moral (or lesson) of this Dreaming story?

   ....

   ....

   ....

Now write!

Research another Dreaming story. Write what happens in the story and the lesson it teaches.

Note: The text is imaginative—a Dreaming story. It has an orientation, a complication, a series of events and a resolution.

Answers and explanations on p. 94

Judgement questions

Use the **Step-by-step guide** on pages 48–49 to help you read the text and make **judgements** to answer the questions below. Circle the correct answers or write your answer on the lines.

Rikki-Tikki-Tavi

Rikki-Tikki-Tavi was a mongoose. He was rather like a little cat in his fur and his tail, but quite like a weasel in his head and his habits. His eyes and the end of his restless nose were pink. He could scratch himself anywhere he pleased with any leg, front or back, that he chose to use. He could fluff up his tail till it looked like a bottle brush.

One day, a high summer flood washed him out of the burrow where he lived with his father and mother, and carried him, kicking and clucking, down a roadside ditch. He found a little wisp of grass floating there, and clung to it till he lost his senses. When he revived, he was lying in the hot sun on the middle of a garden path, very draggled indeed, and a small boy was saying, 'Here's a dead mongoose. Let's have a funeral.'

'No,' said his mother. 'Let's take him in and dry him. Perhaps he isn't really dead.'

From *The Jungle Book* by Rudyard Kipling, 1894

1. The narrator describes the mongoose's nose as *restless* (line 4) to hint that
   - **A** the mongoose sneezes all the time.
   - **B** the mongoose looks funny.
   - **C** the mongoose is a mischievous character.

2. *kicking and clucking* (line 9). What does this tell you about the mongoose?
   - **A** It fought to survive.
   - **B** It is always angry.
   - **C** It is a good swimmer.

3. Which of the following best describes how the mongoose looked when it was on the garden path?
   - **A** hot and bothered
   - **B** wet and battered
   - **C** like a cat with a bottle-brush tail

4. A mongoose is
   - **A** more like a cat than a weasel.
   - **B** more like a weasel than a cat.
   - **C** mostly like a bottle brush.

5. Finish this sentence:
   The high summer flood
   - **A** sounds like fun.
   - **B** sounds dangerous.
   - **C** rarely occurs.

6. What do you think about the boy's reaction to the mongoose?

   ....

   ....

   ....

   ....

Now write!

Write a description of an animal character for a narrative you will write.

Note: The text is imaginative—a narrative.

Answers and explanations on pp. 94–95

Judgement questions

Use the **Step-by-step guide** on pages 48–49 to help you read the text and make **judgements** to answer the questions below. Circle the correct answers or write your answers on the lines.

The Postman

I'd like to be a postman, and walk along the street,
Calling out, 'Good Morning, Sir,' to gentlemen I meet,
Ringing every doorbell all along my beat,
In my cap and uniform so very nice and neat.
Perhaps I'd have a parasol in case of rain or heat;
But I wouldn't be a postman if …
The walking hurt my feet.
Would you?

From *A Book for Kids* by CJ Dennis, 1921

1 How can you tell that this poem was written long ago (1921)?

2 The poet imagines himself as a postman being

A stern.
B bossy.
C polite.

3 The poet imagines he would feel ________________ to wear a postman's uniform.

A proud
B embarrassed
C uncomfortable

4 The main purpose of the poem is

A to amuse the reader.
B to explain what a postman does.
C to show how to be a good postman.

5 What is the effect of ending the poem with *Would you?*

6 Do you think the illustration suits the poem? Why or why not? Explain.

Now write!

What would you like to be when you grow up? Write a poem about it. You could use the same pattern as 'The Postman' or make up a pattern of your own.

Note: The text is imaginative—a poem. It uses rhyme (*street, meet, beat*) except for the third-last line and the final question *Would you?*

Answers and explanations on p. 95

Judgement questions

Use the **Step-by-step guide** on pages 48–49 to help you read the text and make **judgements** to answer the questions below. Circle the correct answers or write your answers on the lines.

Multiculturalism

Mr King: Can anyone tell me what multiculturalism is?

Adriana: It means many cultures together.

Mr King: That's right, Adriana.

Adriana: We went to the multicultural football round at the weekend so that's how I know. My dad was born in Italy.

May Britt: I went to a multicultural festival a while ago. There was dancing and different foods. I tried souvlaki. Yummeee.

Christos: My mum makes souvlaki. It's Greek.

Mr King: Do you think our class is multicultural?

Christos: Yes. I had really good Swedish meatballs at May Britt's house once.

Mr King: How could we work out just how multicultural our class is?

Adriana: We could do a survey.

May Britt: We could do a graph.

Christos: We could list each family's favourite foods.

1. Mr King is
   - A encouraging of his students.
   - B impatient.
   - C strict.
2. What is Christos's attitude?
   - A enthusiastic
   - B unhelpful
   - C bored
3. How does Adriana feel about multiculturalism?
   - A confused
   - B interested
   - C worried
4. Which is the best solution to Mr King's question in line 12?
   - A Adriana's survey
   - B May Britt's graph
   - C Christos's list
5. Would you like to be in Mr King's class? Explain.

   ....

   ....
6. Does it seem that being multicultural is a good thing in the text? Explain.

   ....

   ....

   ....

Now write!

What kind of multicultural event would you like to attend? Give your reasons.

Note: The text is informative—a discussion.

Answers and explanations on pp. 95–96

BRINGING IT ALL TOGETHER

Mixed questions

Use the **Step-by-step guide** on pages 6–7 to help you read the text and then answer the questions below. Circle the correct answers or write your answer on the lines.

My family

I use Cantonese words for my grandparents and call them Por Por and Gong Gong. They live with their dog, Bi Bi. Bi Bi means baby in Cantonese. Bi Bi is a poodle. She is very loving. She likes to sit on people all the time. She sits on your lap if you are seated or on your feet if you are standing. When you walk she gets under your feet and nearly trips you.

Every July Por Por and Gong Gong go back to Hong Kong to visit my Uncle Julius. While they are away Bi Bi comes to live with us. I have to feed and brush her and take her for walks. She is not very well trained. Por Por says she doesn't mind.

by Emily Chan

1. What is the dog's name?
   A Poodle **B** Gong Gong **C** Bi Bi

2. When do Emily's grandparents visit Hong Kong?
   A when Bi Bi stays with the writer
   B in July
   C when they see Uncle Julius

3. The text mainly tells about
   A a dog.
   B Emily's grandparents.
   C walking the dog.

4. What might the dog do on walks? Choose all that apply.
   A misbehave
   B chase birds
   C drag on the leash

5. Give the word a capital letter.

   ....

6. Why do you think Bi Bi isn't well trained?

   ....

   ....

   ....

Now write!

Write about your own family members and the things they do.

Note: The text is informative—a description.

Answers and explanations on p. 96

Mixed questions

Use the **Step-by-step guide** on pages 6–7 to help you read the text and then answer the questions below. Circle the correct answers or write your answers on the lines.

A visit from Mrs Snake

Imagine Mrs Koala's surprise when she peeped down the tree later on and saw Mrs Snake slowly wriggling her way upwards. Oh, she was frightened!

'Go away, Mrs Snake!' she called in a loud voice.

'I've come to nurse the baby; Mrs Magpie sent me.' And Mrs Snake wriggled higher up the tree. Right on to the branch where Mrs Koala sat she came, and coiled herself round the fork.

'I don't want a nurse.' And poor frightened Mrs Koala tried to push the baby's head back in the pouch. But he *would* peep out.

'He's a nice little fellow, and like his daddy,' said Mrs Snake slyly. 'I can take him along on my back for such lovely rides up and down trees and in and out big black holes.'

Extract from *Blinky Bill* by Dorothy Wall, 1933

1 What does Mrs Koala see when she peeps down the tree?

- **A** Baby Koala peeping out.
- **B** Mrs Snake wriggling up.
- **C** Mrs Magpie flying away.

2 Who is speaking in the illustration?

....

3 Which title would suit this text?

- **A** The lucky escape
- **B** Danger
- **C** Baby Koala is taken for a ride

4 Mrs Koala thinks Mrs Snake

- **A** is not to be trusted.
- **B** is to be trusted.
- **C** wants to help her with Baby Koala.

5 Why does the narrator use the word *slyly* (line 13)?

....

....

6 Do you think Mrs Magpie did send Mrs Snake? Explain.

....

....

....

Now write!

Write a story about a visitor who made trouble.

Note: The text is imaginative—a narrative. It uses conversation.

Answers and explanations on p. 96

Mixed questions

Use the **Step-by-step guide** on pages 6–7 to help you read the text and then answer the questions below. Circle the correct answers or write your answers on the lines or in the boxes.

My broken arm

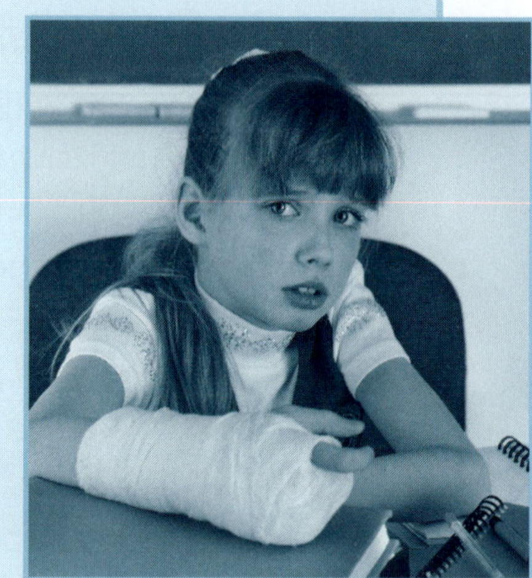

Last Saturday I broke my arm.

I was playing on the monkey bars in the park when my hand slipped and I fell on the ground. At first my arm looked fine but it hurt a lot. Dad took me home and put an icepack on it. He said that would reduce the swelling and I'd be alright. I sat on the sofa and watched some DVDs.

A few hours later my arm was still sore and it started to get a big bruise. Dad took me to the hospital. I had an X-ray. The X-ray was a photo of my arm bones. The doctor said I had a hairline fracture. That's a really thin crack in the bone.

Now I have to wear a cast to keep my bone in place until it mends itself. Stupid monkey bars!

1 What is a hairline fracture?

- A an arm bone
- B a thin crack in a bone
- C a picture of bones on an X-ray

2 Why did Dad use ice?

- A to fix the arm
- B to keep the swelling down
- C to make the arm better

3 Write numbers in the boxes to show the order of events.

- ☐ I fell off the monkey bars.
- ☐ I went to the park.
- ☐ I had an X-ray.
- ☐ I broke my arm.

4 How does the narrator feel about breaking her arm?

- A excited
- B happy
- C disappointed

5 Why is the playground equipment called *monkey bars* (line 3)?

- A Monkeys climb on bars in playgrounds.
- B Children can pretend to be monkeys.
- C Children climb and swing like monkeys.

6 Are the monkey bars *Stupid* (line 13)? Explain.

....

....

....

Now write!

Have you ever broken a bone, hurt yourself or had an accident? Write a recount of the events.

Notes: The text is informative—a personal recount.

Answers and explanations on pp. 96–97

Mixed questions

Use the **Step-by-step guide** on pages 6–7 to help you read the text and then answer the questions below. Circle the correct answers or write your answer on the lines.

Roosters

When male chicks grow up they are called roosters. Most roosters have feathers that are glossy and brightly coloured. The red combs on the roosters' heads are usually larger than the hens' combs. Roosters also have longer tail feathers than hens.

Roosters begin crowing at the crack of dawn. Some breeds of roosters crow through much of the day. Others only crow a few times. Roosters are known for taking care of their female flock.

They crow to tell other roosters to keep out of their territory. They crow to warn their families of danger when they sense a fox or a dog is nearby.

1. The combs on roosters' heads are usually
   - **A** the same size as the hens' combs.
   - **B** smaller than the hens' combs.
   - **C** larger than the hens' combs.
2. Roosters begin crowing
   - **A** at dusk.
   - **B** at dawn.
   - **C** at midday.
3. Roosters' feathers are compared with hens' feathers
   - **A** in the whole text.
   - **B** in paragraph one.
   - **C** in paragraph two.
4. Who is included in a rooster's family?
   - **A** a flock of hens
   - **B** a flock of roosters
   - **C** crows and hens
5. The *crack of dawn* (line 7) means
   - **A** the moment the sun rises.
   - **B** when the sky cracks open.
   - **C** after the sun has been up for a while.
6. In what way are roosters like guards?

   ....

   ....

   ....

   ....

   ....

Now write!

Choose a different animal. Research what they look like and how they behave. Write a report about your animal.

Note: This is an informative text—a report. It uses descriptive words (adjectives and noun groups) and makes comparisons to tell what an animal looks like and how it behaves.

Answers and explanations on p. 97

Mixed questions

Use the **Step-by-step guide** on pages 6–7 to help you read the text and then answer the questions below. Circle the correct answers or write your answer on the lines.

Eddie's question

Eddie called out from the lounge room, 'Hey Mum! Mario's dad is taking Mario to see his sister play the drums. There's a concert at her high school on Friday night. Can I go with them? Mario's dad's invited me. It finishes at 9 pm. He said I'll get home before 9.30. He's going to pick me up here at 5.30. Or I can go home from school with Mario on Friday. They're having Thai for dinner before the concert. It's Mario's sister's favourite. He said for you to phone him tonight or tomorrow. Or you can talk with him on Friday if he collects me from here. Is that OK?'

Mum entered the lounge room. 'Say all that again,' she said.

1. Who plays drums?
   - A Eddie
   - B Mario
   - C Mario's sister

2. What time does the concert finish?
   - A 5.30 pm
   - B 9 pm
   - C 9.30 pm

3. What event led to Eddie's invitation from Mario's dad?
   - A Eddie's mum can phone Mario's dad.
   - B Mario's sister was selected to play in the concert.
   - C Eddie can walk home from school with Mario on Friday.

4. Why are they having Mario's sister's favourite food?
   - A There's nowhere else to eat.
   - B It's her special night.
   - C Mario likes Thai too.

5. *He said for you to phone him tonight or tomorrow* (lines 9–10).

   Who is *He*?
   - A Mario
   - B Mario's dad
   - C the writer

6. Do you think Eddie will be allowed to go? Explain.

   ....

   ....

   ....

Now write!

Write a conversation you might have with a family member. Ask for permission to do something. Write the family member's response. Use direct speech.

Note: The text is informative—a conversation. The text includes quoted and reported speech.

Answers and explanations on p. 97

Mixed questions

Use the **Step-by-step guide** on pages 6–7 to help you read the text and then answer the questions below. Circle the correct answers or write your answer on the lines.

A bluebottle sting

Last Sunday a bluebottle stung me. It *really* hurt.

Mum and I went to the beach with Dad. He is a volunteer surf lifesaver so he was on duty.

I'd been in the water for a while when I felt a horrible, burning pain. I spotted a bluebottle floating near me. Its long tentacle was wrapped around my arm.

I ran out of the water yelling for Dad. He said not to try to get the tentacle off with my hand. He splashed it off with sea water and then he used plastic tweezers to pull the last bit off.

The pain was horrible. It lasted for ages but a heat pack helped a bit. Dad said people used to use ice packs but the latest research says hot water or a heat pack works best.

I'll look out for bluebottles before I go in the water next time. Dad just said I was unlucky as there were hardly any bluebottles around that day.

by Ella

1. You wash off a tentacle with
   - **A** ice water.
   - **B** sea water.
   - **C** vinegar.

2. Where was Ella stung?
   - **A** on her leg
   - **B** on her arm
   - **C** on her foot

3. What do you do first to treat a bluebottle sting?
   - **A** use a heat pack
   - **B** run out of the water
   - **C** wash off the tentacle with sea water

4. How do you treat pain from a bluebottle sting?
   - **A** with heat
   - **B** with ice
   - **C** with sea water

5. What does *the latest research* *(line 15)* mean?
   - **A** what many people think
   - **B** the most recent study of the subject
   - **C** the dad's opinion

6. How did Ella's dad react to Ella's problem? Explain.

....

....

Now write!

Write about a time when you were hurt. What happened? How did you get better?

Note: The text is informative—a personal recount. The writer gives her point of view about events.

Answers and explanations on pp. 97–98

Mixed questions

Use the **Step-by-step guide** on pages 6–7 to help you read the text and then answer the questions below. Circle the correct answers or write your answers on the lines.

Furry lifesaver

Budapest News 19.6.23

Visitors to Budapest Zoo were amazed when a huge bear rescued a crow from drowning in its enclosure.

The crow had fallen into the bear's moat. It flapped its wet wings and struggled to get back into the air but it was doomed to drown.

The bear watched it for a moment. Then the bear lumbered over. It stuck its paw into the water, scooped the crow into its mouth by a wing tip then lifted the crow out of the water and onto the dirt.

The surprised crow rested for a moment then stood up. It was wet and muddy but unharmed.

It's not surprising that the bear showed kindness towards the bird. There are always news stories about different species helping each other.

1 Why did the crow need help?

A A bear was trying to eat it.

B It was drowning.

C It was wet and muddy.

2 What part of the bear lifted the crow onto the dirt?

....

3 Choose a different title for the text.

A Budapest Zoo

B Bear saves crow

C A wet and muddy crow

4 What is the writer's opinion of events?

A surprised

B not surprised

C amazed

5 *lumbered* **(line 10)**

What does this verb mean?

A rushed quickly

B walked carefully

C moved heavily

6 Why do you think the bear helped the crow?

....

....

....

Now write!

Write an item of news about something that's happening in your area.

Note: The text is informative—an online news article. The text recounts events in logical order and gives a point of view.

Answers and explanations on p. 98

Mixed questions

Use the **Step-by-step guide** on pages 6–7 to help you read the text and then answer the questions below. Circle the correct answers or write your answers on the lines.

The Great Mango Mystery

Once upon a time, in the kingdom of Desa Kiara, all the mangoes had disappeared. Phhht. Gone! This made the people of the kingdom cross and grumpy. They told young Prince Jason their troubles. He'd solve the mystery if anybody could.

Prince Jason searched every centimetre of the kingdom. No mangoes! All of a sudden he remembered his mother, Queen Snow, and his father, King Akmal, loved eating mangoes. Had they gobbled them up?

He practised his sternest face in front of the mirror. Now he was ready to confront his parents.

'Did you steal all the mangoes?' he asked in his steeliest voice.

'Yes,' they trembled.

'You must share the mangoes with everyone,' Prince Jason said severely.

'Certainly, dearest Jason. We promise we'll never do it again,' his parents replied.

Prince Jason was hailed as a hero. The Great Mango Mystery was solved and they all lived happily ever after.

1. The character *hailed as a hero* **(line 17)** was

   ....

2. Why were the people of Desa Kiara *cross and grumpy* **(line 4)**?
   - **A** All the mangoes had disappeared.
   - **B** Prince Jason couldn't find the missing mangoes.
   - **C** The people were very hungry.

3. The story is mainly about
   - **A** greed.
   - **B** the importance of sharing.
   - **C** telling lies.

4. Why did Queen Snow and King Akmal tremble **(line 14)**?
   - **A** They were guilty and had been found out.
   - **B** They had grown old and shaky.
   - **C** They were trembling with rage because they had been found out.

5. The word *confront* **(line 12)** means
   - **A** move to the front.
   - **B** say something unkind.
   - **C** face with the truth.

6. Do you think Prince Jason is a hero? Explain.

   ....

   ....

Now write!

Write a mystery story.

Note: The text is imaginative—a narrative.

Answers and explanations on p. 98

Mixed questions

Use the **Step-by-step guide** on pages 6–7 to help you read the text and then answer the questions below. Circle the correct answers or write your answers on the lines.

Stay away!

Maggie and Marty sat on a branch guarding their nest in the tree above the kindergarten. They happily shared their territory with the kindy children. Last year's chicks liked the kindy children and begged the children for food. But Marty did not like people cycling past the kindy, on the footpath outside kindy, during nesting season. These were people he did not know. These people were a threat to the chicks.

Marty spotted someone on a bicycle. Marty swooped. *Clack clack*! snapped his beak loudly. That would teach the cyclist to stay away, thought Maggie. Good job, Marty! She looked at her three newly hatched magpie chicks. They'd need her and Marty to protect them for a few weeks yet. They were so defenceless.

1 What is Maggie?

....

2 Where do Maggie and Marty live?

A at the kindergarten

B in trees above a kindergarten

C on a nest

3 Why did Marty swoop the cyclist?

A He was protecting his nest.

B He hates cyclists.

C He always defends his territory.

4 *Stay away!* **(line 1)** Who thinks this?

A a cyclist

B a magpie

C kindy children

5 What does *defenceless* **(line 16)** mean?

A protective

B resisting attack

C open to danger

6 What do you think of Marty's behaviour?

....

....

....

....

....

Now write!

Write an animal story. Give the animals names and personalities.

Note: The text is imaginative—a narrative. Animal characters are given human feelings.

Answers and explanations on pp. 98–99

Mixed questions

Use the **Step-by-step guide** on pages 6–7 to help you read the text and then answer the questions below. Circle the correct answers or write your answers on the lines.

What is a cloud?

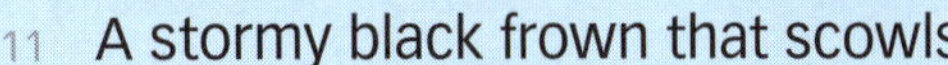

A cloud is
something to look down on
when I'm in a plane or on a mountain;
a soft, white pillow to lay my head on;
a bouncy mattress for me to play with.
Millions of water droplets
tossing in the air.
Something to look up to
on a winter's day.
A stormy black frown that scowls
at upturned faces.
A lonely white wisp
drifting across the sky
hoping to find a friend.

1. How many water droplets make up a cloud?

2. What colour are the storm clouds in this poem?
   A black
   B grey
   C white

3. The clouds in the poem are viewed from
   A different positions.
   B the same position.
   C inside.

4. Why do the people turn their faces up?
   A They are looking to see if it is beginning to rain.
   B They are turning up their noses at the rain.
   C They are hoping it won't rain.

5. What does the word *lonely* suggest about the *white wisp* of cloud *(line 13)*?

6. What attitude does the poet have towards clouds? Explain.

Now write!

Write a poem about something in nature that you admire. What is it? What does it look like? What does it do? How does it make you feel?

Note: The text is imaginative—a poem. It expresses personal thoughts and feelings about a subject.

Answers and explanations on p. 99

Mixed questions

Use the **Step-by-step guide** on pages 6–7 to help you read the text and then answer the questions below. Circle the correct answers or write your answers on the lines.

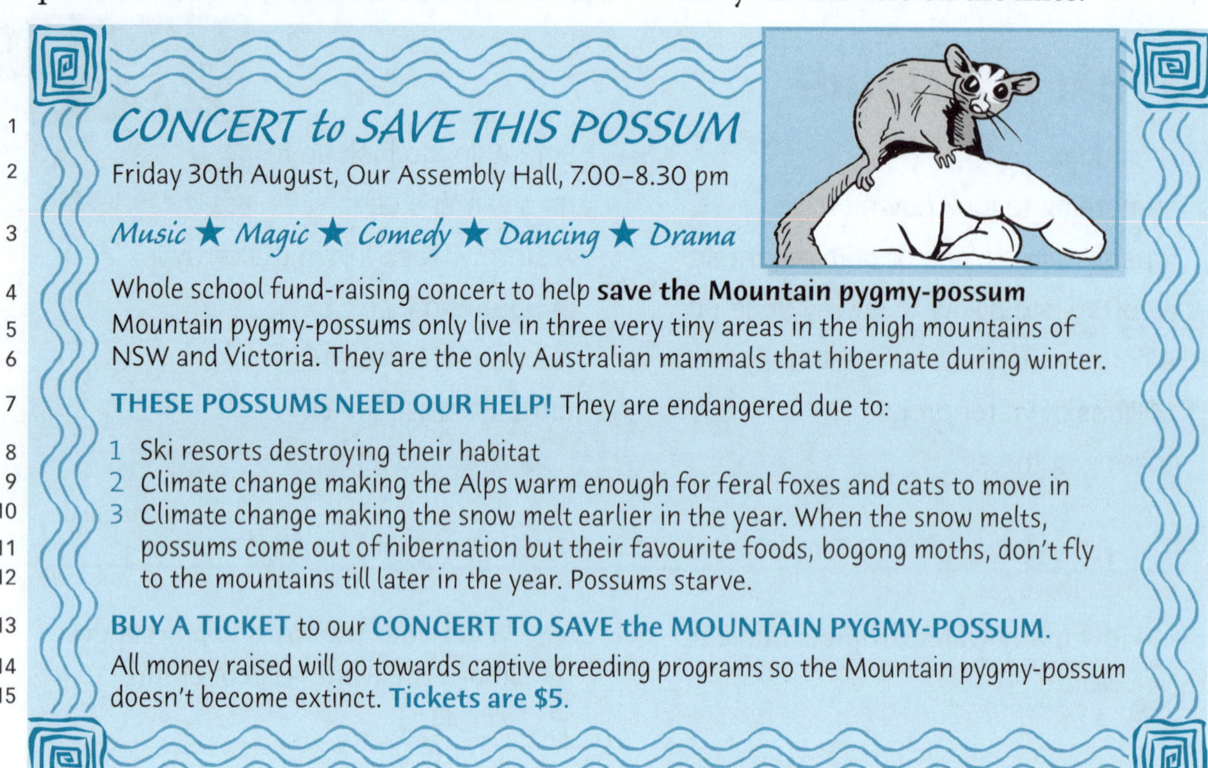

CONCERT to SAVE THIS POSSUM

Friday 30th August, Our Assembly Hall, 7.00–8.30 pm

Music ★ Magic ★ Comedy ★ Dancing ★ Drama

Whole school fund-raising concert to help **save the Mountain pygmy-possum** Mountain pygmy-possums only live in three very tiny areas in the high mountains of NSW and Victoria. They are the only Australian mammals that hibernate during winter.

THESE POSSUMS NEED OUR HELP! They are endangered due to:

1 Ski resorts destroying their habitat
2 Climate change making the Alps warm enough for feral foxes and cats to move in
3 Climate change making the snow melt earlier in the year. When the snow melts, possums come out of hibernation but their favourite foods, bogong moths, don't fly to the mountains till later in the year. Possums starve.

BUY A TICKET to our **CONCERT TO SAVE the MOUNTAIN PYGMY-POSSUM.**

All money raised will go towards captive breeding programs so the Mountain pygmy-possum doesn't become extinct. **Tickets are $5.**

1 Where do Mountain pygmy-possums live?

....

2 Concert money will be used for

A music at the concert.

B captive breeding programs.

C food for the possums.

3 What is the purpose of the text?

A to advertise concert tickets

B to advertise ways to help the possums

C to inform people about the possums

4 What kills possums?

A bogong moths

B cats and foxes

C hunters

5 What is *THIS POSSUM* in the title *CONCERT to SAVE THIS POSSUM*?

A the possum in the drawing

B the Mountain pygmy-possum

C pygmy-possums

6 Do you think this poster does a good job? Explain.

....

....

....

Now write!

Make a poster to inform people about an upcoming event at your school.

Note: The text is informative—a poster. It uses technical terms.

Answers and explanations on p. 99

Mixed questions

Use the **Step-by-step guide** on pages 6–7 to help you read the text and then answer the questions below. Circle the correct answers or write your answer on the lines.

Animal sounds

Animals use sounds to 'talk' to each other. People often use onomatopoeic* words for the sounds animals make. We say, for example, that elephants trumpet, mice squeak, frogs croak, roosters say cock-a-doodle-do and cats miaow.

Animals make sounds that warn of danger. They make sounds to report where to find food. Some animals, such as bats, make sounds to find each other in the dark.

Different species of animals make different sounds. Cockatoos make sounds like cars screeching to a halt. They also copy human speech. Parrots and budgerigars copy human speech too. A bellbird's song sounds like bells ringing a melody.

Some animals make sounds without using their voices. Crickets and cicadas, for example, can make sounds by rubbing their body parts.

*Words that sound like the thing or sound they are describing.

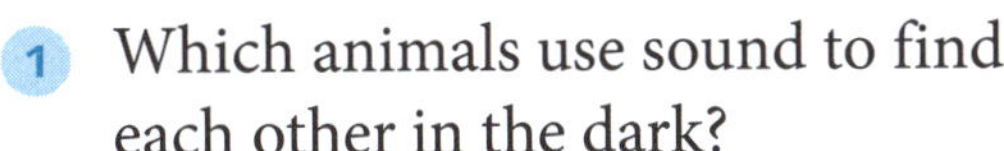

1. Which animals use sound to find each other in the dark?
   - A snails
   - B bats
   - C roosters
2. Which animals copy human speech? Choose all that apply.
   - A cockatoos
   - B budgerigars
   - C parrots
3. What is the main idea in the text?
   - A Animals can talk to people.
   - B Animals use sounds to communicate.
   - C Animals make sounds.
4. Animals of the same species make
   - A similar sounds to each other.
   - B different sounds from each other.
   - C no sounds.
5. Which word is the odd one out?
   - A squeak
   - B bells
   - C croak
6. Which animal in the text do you think makes the cleverest sound? Explain.

   ....

   ....

   ....

Now write!

Make up a song that includes animal sounds.

Note: The text is informative—a report. It gives factual information with examples.

Answers and explanations on pp. 99–100

Mixed questions

Use the **Step-by-step guide** on pages 6–7 to help you read the text and then answer the questions below. Circle the correct answers or write your answer on the lines.

Burketown Times, July 2007

Bones of giant animal found

Scientists have found the bones of a very large animal, a diprotodon. The bones were dug up in far northern Queensland.

'We are pleased because we found the skull and jaws and most of the rest of the skeleton. It is rare to find whole diprotodon skeletons,' the team leader said. 'This animal was probably around the size of a small car.'

Scientists believe that diprotodons looked like giant wombats. They became extinct about 55 000 years ago after living on earth for around two and a half million years.

'Climate change, a flood or overhunting may have caused their disappearance. We are still trying to find out,' the team leader added.

More bones of giant-sized animals, such as those of giant kangaroos and lizards, have been discovered near the site.

1 Where were the bones of the diprotodon found?

A southern Queensland

B far northern Queensland

C Queensland

2 What did diprotodons look like?

A giants

B small cars

C giant wombats

3 The main purpose of the text is to

A report the discovery of the bones of a giant-sized animal.

B describe diprotodons.

C tell a story about diprotodons.

4 How many bones of the diprotodon were found?

A the complete skeleton

B a small number

C most of the skeleton

5 *Bones of giant animal found* **(line 2)**

The word *giant* suggests that

A the bones are not real bones.

B the report is a fairytale.

C the bones found were from an extra-large animal.

6 Do you think scientists will continue to dig in the area? Explain.

....

....

....

Write a newspaper report about a discovery.

Note: The text is informative—a newspaper article. It includes quotations from a scientist.

Answers and explanations on p. 100

Mixed questions

Use the **Step-by-step guide** on pages 6–7 to help you read the text and then answer the questions below. Circle the correct answers or write your answer on the line.

Tonsillectomy

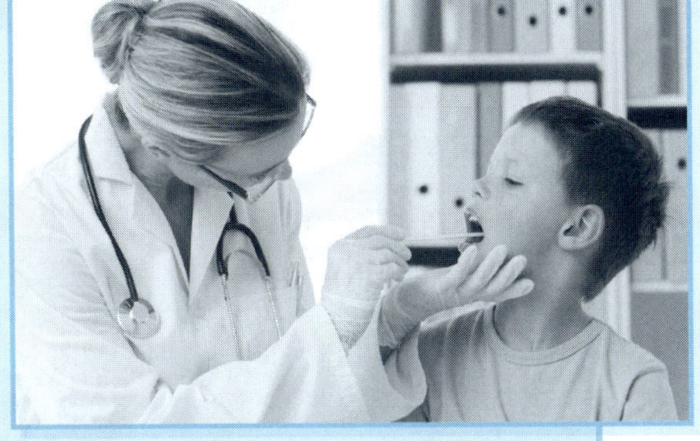

Bonjour.

Hello Pépère. I have to get my tonsils out.

Ah, Jean Pierre, you have a problem with your tonsils, yes?

Yes. I keep getting infections and missing school.

Well then. I believe this tonsil removal is a good thing. No?

Yes. My tonsils are really big. They get in the way of my breathing. I breathe through my mouth instead of my nose and it wakes me up at night. The operation is on Friday of next week. I might have to stay in hospital for one night.

Ah, that sounds like fun. You will have a little holiday.

Well not really, Pépère. I'm having an operation and I'll have a sore throat.

Well then you will need ice-creams. Put your mother on the phone for me, please. A grandfather's job is to make sure you have many ice-creams for your sore throat.

1 The conversation is between
- A a child and his grandfather.
- B a boy and his doctor.
- C a parent and child.

2 What is a reason for having tonsils taken out?
- A They choke you.
- B You get too many infections.
- C They are too big.

3 Which statement belongs next in the text?
- A The operation is on Friday of next week.
- B Open wide and let me look at your throat.
- C Bonjour my daughter.

4 What sort of relationship do the speakers have?
- A difficult because English is Pépère's second language
- B awkward because they live far apart
- C loving and close

5 What is a tonsillectomy?
- A a hospital that takes out tonsils
- B an operation to remove tonsils
- C a tonsil infection

6 How does Pépère feel about the operation?

....

Now write!

Find a partner to work with. Act out a telephone conversation about a topic of your choice. Then write the conversation.

Note: The text is informative—a conversation. It shows relationships within a family.

Answers and explanations on p. 100

Mixed questions

Use the **Step-by-step guide** on pages 6–7 to help you read the text and then answer the questions below. Circle the correct answers or write your answer on the lines.

Wipe-out!

Wipe-out!

The new soap-in-a-bottle.

Wipes out germs with powerful germ-fighting ingredients.

Buy now.

Your family can be healthy and germ-free for just a few cents a day.

See Wipe-out! in action at your local chemist or supermarket today.

We'll use Light-up! germ gel and UV light to show you the germs on your hands. Then Wipe-out! will make them disappear! **SEE** the difference.

Our promise to you: Germs are wiped out!

Say goodbye to germs with Wipe-out!

Children will love the germ monster stickers, free with every purchase.

1. What is *Wipe-out!*?
   - **A** germ-fighting ingredients
   - **B** a free sticker
   - **C** soap-in-a-bottle
2. How much does *Wipe-out!* cost?
   - **A** a few cents each day
   - **B** five dollars a month
   - **C** about a dollar a week
3. What does the text want people to do?
   - **A** buy *Wipe-out!*
   - **B** kill germs
   - **C** collect stickers
4. How does *Wipe-out!* work?
   - **A** It's a soap-in-a-bottle.
   - **B** It uses *Light-up!* germ gel.
   - **C** It has powerful ingredients to kill germs.
5. The name *Wipe-out!* sounds
   - **A** powerful.
   - **B** healthy.
   - **C** expensive.
6. Would you like to try *Wipe-out!*? Explain your reasons.

   ....

   ....

   ....

Now write!

Invent a product and design an advertisement for a magazine.

Note: The text is persuasive—an advertisement. It uses commands and free gifts to sell a product.

Answers and explanations on pp. 100–101

Mixed questions

Use the **Step-by-step guide** on pages 6–7 to help you read the text and then answer the questions below. Circle the correct answers or write your answers on the lines.

The herd

Savannah was the herd's leader, the matriarch. All eyes turned towards her. How would she deal with Lox? Would she allow him to stay with the females and youngsters any longer? He was now the oldest teenage male. It was his time to leave the herd. He was strong and fit.

Savannah gave him a gentle nudge with her trunk. He needed to be on his way. He could live with other young bulls, if he wanted to, or roam on his own. That was the way of the bulls. The herd sometimes saw Lox's older brother, Chad, and his cousins at the waterhole. Lox could join them.

Savannah nudged him again, coaxing him away from the herd.

1. The main elephant in the story is
   - **A** Lox.
   - **B** Chad.
   - **C** Savannah.

2. What is the name for a group of elephants?

   ....

3. What do you expect to happen next?
   - **A** Savannah will get angry with Lox.
   - **B** Lox will stay with the herd.
   - **C** Lox will leave the herd.

4. Which statement is true in the text?
   - **A** Male elephants live at waterholes.
   - **B** Young bull elephants prefer to roam on their own.
   - **C** Female elephants live in herds.

5. *Matriarch* is a name for
   - **A** the female head of a family.
   - **B** the king of the herd.
   - **C** an adult elephant.

6. Was Savannah worried about Lox leaving the herd? Explain.

   ....

   ....

   ....

   ....

   ....

Now write!

Write an animal story. Do research first so you can base the story on facts about the way the animals live.

Note: The text is imaginative—a narrative. It is written in the third person. It presents an animal's point of view.

Answers and explanations on p. 101

Mixed questions

Use the **Step-by-step guide** on pages 6–7 to help you read the text and then answer the questions below. Circle the correct answers or write your answer on the lines.

Sandy's Animal Shelter

4th June

We need more volunteers

There are just too many animals for the staff at the shelter to look after. Some days we don't even have time to pat the animals. We just clean kennels and wash dishes.

Comments

Staff need the help of volunteers just as much as the animals do.

I know volunteers like to walk the dogs. Please don't neglect the cats. They need attention too.

1st June

Older animals need homes too

It's difficult to rehome older animals. People choose puppies and kittens rather than older animals. That's heartbreaking.

Comments

Those older animals get so confused. They don't know why they are at the shelter. They did have families once.

5th May

Blankets needed

It's getting colder. We need blankets at the shelter. There's a blanket drive for the beginning of winter.

Archive

Tags

Blogroll

Links

1. Staff at the shelter
   - **A** did have families once.
   - **B** clean kennels and wash dishes.
   - **C** play with animals all day.
2. When choosing pets most people prefer
   - **A** dogs that they can walk.
   - **B** older animals.
   - **C** puppies and kittens.
3. What is the blog about?
   - **A** animals at a shelter
   - **B** cats and dogs
   - **C** an animal shelter
4. Why was the shelter having a blanket drive?
   - **A** Staff feel the cold.
   - **B** Animals feel the cold.
   - **C** Staff and animals feel the cold.
5. What does *neglect* *(line 9)* mean?
   A lose **B** ignore **C** hurt
6. How do workers at the shelter feel about the animals?

   ....

   ....

   ....

Now write!

Create a poster to encourage people to volunteer at an animal shelter.

Note: The text is informative—a blog. It shares points of views about animal welfare and responsible pet ownership.

Answers and explanations on p. 101

Mixed questions

Use the **Step-by-step guide** on pages 6–7 to help you read the text and then answer the questions below. Circle the correct answers or write your answers on the lines.

Grandpa's school report

This is Grandpa's report from when he was in Year Two.

Primrose Primary School **Yearly Report**
Name: *Jim Brown*
Date: *December 1956*

Subject	Result	Comment
Maths	*C*	*Jim could probably do better. He needs to try harder.*
English	*C*	*Jim should try harder.*
Science	*C*	*Jim spends too much time dreaming in class.*
Art	*A*	*Jim's drawing is excellent. He works very hard.*

General comment
Jim must leave his animals at home. School is not the place for mice or guinea pigs.
Signed: *Peter Raff*
Year *Two* Form Master

1 Who is this report about?

....

2 In which subject did Jim work very hard?
- A Maths
- B Science
- C Art

3 *Jim did not participate in community work this term.*

Where could this sentence be added?
- A with the General comment
- B with the Science comment
- C with thc Maths commcnt

4 Which is likely to be Jim's favourite subject?
- A English
- B Art
- C Science

5 Which statement is the most definite?
- A Jim could probably do better.
- B Jim should try harder.
- C Jim must leave his animals at home.

6 Do you think the Form Master liked Jim? Explain.

....

....

....

....

Now write!

Imagine you are a teacher. Write a school report for yourself.

Note: The text is informative—a school report. It uses evaluative language.

Answers and explanations on p. 102

Mixed questions

Use the **Step-by-step guide** on pages 6–7 to help you read the text and then answer the questions below. Circle the correct answers or write your answers on the lines.

Rufus

This is me with my dog, Rufus. Rufus means red. We got him from the animal shelter. His owners had moved from a house to a home unit and couldn't take Rufus with them.

Rufus was already an old dog when we got him. He was twelve. Dad said he was no spring chicken but he was in good health so we took him home with us.

Mum says it's good to give a pet a second chance at a good home. Sometimes I wonder whether Rufus misses his old family and whether they miss their furry red dog. Then I feel sad for him.

Jasmine and Rufus

1. Who wrote the text?

   ....

2. Why didn't Rufus's old owners keep him?
   - **A** They wanted to find him a good home.
   - **B** They moved from a house to a unit.
   - **C** They didn't want him.

3. Sequence the events in Rufus's life.

   First: ____ Second: ____ Third: ____
   - **A** Jasmine found Rufus at the animal shelter.
   - **B** Rufus was left at the animal shelter.
   - **C** Rufus went to live with Jasmine.

4. How did Rufus get his name?
   - **A** He got his name at the animal shelter.
   - **B** He has red fur.
   - **C** Jasmine named him.

5. *he was no spring chicken* (line 6).

   What does this mean?
   - **A** He was not a young dog.
   - **B** He was quite a young dog.
   - **C** He was a dog and not a chicken.

6. Why does Jasmine sometimes feel sad about Rufus?
   - **A** Rufus feels abandoned.
   - **B** Rufus is old.
   - **C** She imagines what Rufus might be thinking.

Now write!

Imagine being a dog left at an animal shelter. How would you feel?

....

....

....

....

Note: The text is informative—a personal response. It presents the writer's point of view.

Answers and explanations on p. 102

Mixed questions

Use the **Step-by-step guide** on pages 6–7 to help you read the text and then answer the questions below. Circle the correct answers or write your answer on the lines.

My friend from Iraq

My friend Hariq escaped from the war in Iraq. He came to Australia with his mother, his father and his sister. They were refugees. When he got here he had nothing—only the clothes he had on, but he says he was lucky.

Hariq told me that at first school work in Australia was very difficult. He hadn't been to school very often in Iraq. He couldn't read or write very much in his own language. He didn't speak any English either. Then he met my dad.

My dad is a homework volunteer. He spends one afternoon a week helping children like Hariq do their homework at the Homework Centre, after school. All the children are refugees. They have come to Australia from faraway places like Iraq, Afghanistan, Somalia and Sri Lanka. Now they call Australia home. Hariq is Dad's star pupil.

1. Name five countries in the text.

   ....

   ....

   ....

   ....

2. When Hariq arrived in Australia he was
   - **A** a volunteer.
   - **B** the writer's friend.
   - **C** a refugee.

3. The text is about
   - **A** Hariq and Iraq.
   - **B** the writer's dad.
   - **C** the writer's friend Hariq.

4. Since Hariq met the writer's dad
   - **A** school work is no longer very difficult.
   - **B** he doesn't need to go to school any more.
   - **C** he has become a refugee.

5. What does *refugee* mean in the text?
   - **A** a child who comes from a faraway place
   - **B** someone who escapes to a new country for safety
   - **C** people from Iraq, like Hariq

6. What does the writer think about his dad being a homework volunteer?
   - **A** surprised
   - **B** proud and interested
   - **C** jealous

Now write!

Imagine arriving in a new country with nothing. How would you feel?

Note: The text is informative—a personal response.

Answers and explanations on p. 102

Mixed questions

Use the **Step-by-step guide** on pages 6–7 to help you read the text and then answer the questions below. Circle the correct answers or write your answers on the lines.

The punishment

There was once a king who thought he was clever. He did things that made the Greek gods very angry. The god of the underworld came up to earth. He brought handcuffs with him to capture the king but instead the king tricked the god. The god put his own hands into the handcuffs and the king escaped.

It took many years but the god of the underworld finally caught the king. He took the king down to the underworld to be punished. The king was given a task to complete. He was told to push a great rock to the top of a hill. However, when he got the rock to the top of the hill, the rock rolled back down. Then the king had to push it up the hill all over again. The king never completed his task. The god of the underworld had his revenge.

1. Who did the king anger?

   ....

2. What did the god use to try to capture the king?
   - **A** rope
   - **B** handcuffs
   - **C** poison

3. Which of these events happened first?
   - **A** The god punished the king.
   - **B** The king tricked the god.
   - **C** The king escaped.

4. How did the king feel about the Greek gods?
   - **A** He was unafraid of them.
   - **B** He admired them.
   - **C** He looked up to them.

5. Which word could replace the phrase *all over again* **(line 14)**?
   - **A** repeatedly
   - **B** quickly
   - **C** often

6. Why did the god give the king such a nasty punishment?

   ....

   ....

   ....

Now write!

What punishment do you receive if you break a rule? Explain.

Note: This is an imaginative text—a narrative. It is a Greek legend. It is told in the third person and is in the past tense.

Answers and explanations on p. 103

Mixed questions

Use the **Step-by-step guide** on pages 6–7 to help you read the text and then answer the questions below. Circle the correct answers or write your answers on the lines.

Animal dads

The seahorse

The seahorse is a fish. The mother seahorse lays hundreds of eggs in the father's pouch. The eggs hatch inside his pouch. The tiny fry fend for themselves after they leave the pouch.

The Emperor penguin

The Emperor penguin is a bird. The mother lays one egg onto her feet. Then she shifts the egg onto the father penguin's feet. They don't let the egg touch the ice. The father keeps the egg warm with his pouch. The egg hatches in two months. The mother penguin comes back to feed her chick.

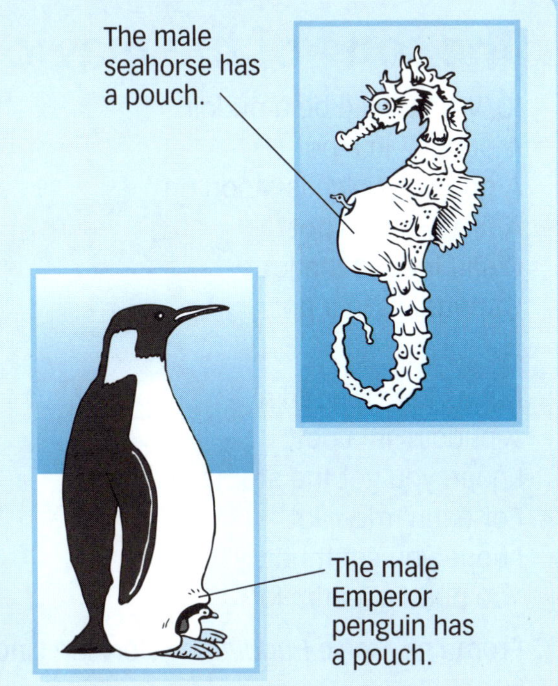

1. What are baby seahorses called?

   ....

2. What is a baby penguin called?

   ....

3. What is the main idea in both texts?
   - **A** animal babies
   - **B** animals that lay eggs
   - **C** animal dads

4. Why can't the egg touch the ice?
   - **A** It mustn't get wet.
   - **B** The cold will crack it.
   - **C** It will make the ice crack.

5. What is a *pouch* ***(lines 4 and 13)*** and what is it for?

   ....

   ....

6. Why do you think a seahorse has hundreds of babies but an Emperor penguin only has one?

   ....

   ....

   ....

   ....

   ....

Now write!

Find out about another animal dad that cares for its young (e.g. the marsupial frog, the arowana fish or the rhea). Write a report.

Note: This is an informative text—a report.

Answers and explanations on p. 103

Mixed questions

Use the **Step-by-step guide** on pages 6–7 to help you read the text and then answer the questions below. Circle the correct answers or write your answer on the line.

The song of the magic pudding

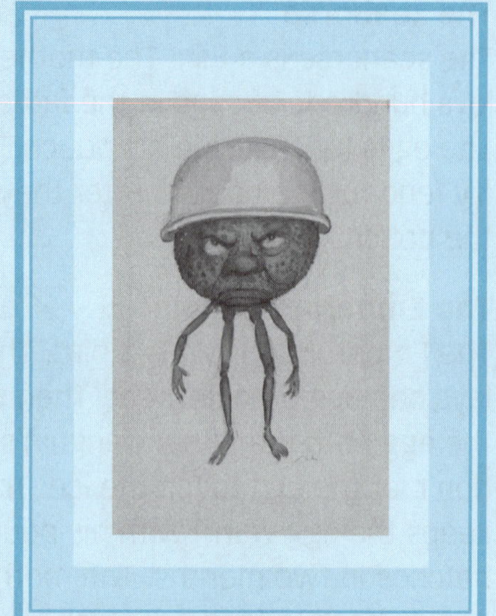

'O, who would be a puddin',
A puddin' in a pot,
A puddin' which is stood on
A fire which is hot?
O sad indeed the lot
Of puddin's in a pot.
...
But as I am a puddin',
A puddin' in a pot,
I hope you get the stomach ache
For eatin' me a lot.
I hope you get it hot,
You puddin'-eatin' lot!'

From *The Magic Pudding* by Norman Lindsay, 1918

Thanks to HC & A Glad for permission to quote from *The Magic Pudding* and for use of the illustration.

1 What is the puddin' in?

....

2 What is the puddin' stood on?

A a stove **B** a fire **C** a bench

3 What is the puddin's purpose in singing its song?

A to give information
B to tell a story
C to make a complaint

4 Why does the puddin' look cross and sad in the illustration?

A It is annoyed about being a puddin'.
B It doesn't like its hat.
C It wants to frighten the reader.

5 Which adjective describes how it feels to be a puddin' in a pot?

A hot **B** sad **C** happy

6 Why does the puddin' hope that the people who eat it get a stomach ache?

A because it is a nasty, mean puddin'
B because it wants to punish them for eating it
C because it is in a grumpy mood

Now write!

Write a poem or a story about a character that has magical powers.

Note: This is an imaginative text—a poem about being a magic pudding. It is written in the first person in the voice of the pudding. It talks in a rough, informal way, dropping the 'g' off the end of its words (*puddin'* for pudding; *eatin'* for eating). Notice that an apostrophe (') is used to replace the missing letters.

Answers and explanations on p. 103

Mixed questions

Use the **Step-by-step guide** on pages 6–7 to help you read the text and then answer the questions below. Circle the correct answers or write your answer on the lines.

Dinosaurs

A dinosaur fossil

Dinosaurs lived on earth a very long time ago. By the time humans lived on earth, dinosaurs had become extinct. How, then, do we know anything about dinosaurs?

Dinosaur fossils are the answer. A fossil is rock that shows evidence of life from long ago. Dinosaur fossils give us evidence of dinosaur bones and skeletons, eggshells and nests, as well as footprints and other impressions. Dinosaur fossils have been found all over the world.

Paleontology is the study of fossils. Dinosaur fossils tell paleontologists about dinosaurs; their sizes and shapes and how they moved. Fossils of dinosaur teeth tell what kinds of food different dinosaurs ate. For example, plant eaters had blunt teeth. Where fossils are found can tell about the environments the dinosaurs lived in.

Without fossils we'd know nothing at all about dinosaurs!

1. When did dinosaurs live on earth?
   - **A** not long ago.
   - **B** a while ago.
   - **C** a very long time ago.
2. Dinosaurs lived on earth
   - **A** before humans.
   - **B** after humans.
   - **C** at the same time as humans.
3. The main idea in the text is
   - **A** what fossils are.
   - **B** how we know about dinosaurs.
   - **C** how dinosaurs became extinct.
4. A fossil of a long sharp tooth would show that the dinosaur ate
   - **A** insects.
   - **B** plants.
   - **C** animals.
5. A paleontologist is a person who studies
   - **A** extinct things.
   - **B** living things.
   - **C** fossils.
6. Would you like to be a paleontologist? Explain.

....

....

....

....

....

Now write!

Research and write a report about an animal that has become extinct.

Note. The text is informative—an explanation. It explains how we get information about the past. It uses technical language related to fossils.

Answers and explanations on pp. 103–104

SECTION 3 ANSWERS

Fact-finding questions

School holidays (page 10)

1 B	**2** B	**3** A	**4** C
5 C	**6** See below		

Explanations

1. This is a **fact-finding** question. **B** is correct. You read *I can stay with you the whole two weeks* (see lines 5–6). **A** is incorrect. Sunday is the day Dad will return to Nan's to collect Ellie. **C** is incorrect as Ellie's parents will *only stay for the weekend* (see lines 6–7).
2. This is a **fact-finding** question. **B** is correct. You read *Then Dad will come back to get me on the Sunday before school goes back* (see lines 7–8). **A** is incorrect. Saturday is the day they will drive up to Nan's. **C** is incorrect. After the weekend is when Ellie's mum and dad will drive home.
3. This is a **fact-finding** question. **A** is correct. You read *Can we also make the boiled pineapple fruit cake? Dad likes that best* (see lines 12–13). **B** is incorrect: *a sometime food* (see line 15) is the expression used by Ellie for cake. **C** is incorrect. Ellie's mother likes scones.
4. This is a **fact-finding** question. **C** is correct. You read *Can we do more cooking?* (see line 9) This is an activity that Ellie likes to do with Nan. **A** and **B** are incorrect. There is nothing in the text to tell you that Ellie does these things with Nan.
5. This is a **fact-finding** question. **C** is correct. You read *I told him* [Dad] *how much fruit was in it and that it had very little sugar* (see lines 13–14). **A** and **B** are each only part of the answer and not the full answer.
6. This is a **fact-finding** question. Ellie will go by car to her nan's. You read *Mum says we'll drive up Saturday* (see lines 4–5).

Not for sale (page 11)

1 C	**2** A	**3** C	**4** B
5 B	**6** See below		

Explanations

1. This is a **fact-finding** question. **C** is correct. You read the note and see that it is *Signed Steven Short* (see line 17). You read *Why did you write that note, Steven?* (see line 2). **A** is incorrect because Dad didn't know about the note. **B** is incorrect because Lou asked Steven why he wrote the note.
2. This is a **fact-finding** question. **A** is correct. You read *Please don't buy our island home* (see lines 14–15). **B** is incorrect. The note does not ask people to buy the house. This is the opposite of what the note says. **C** is incorrect because the note is not about selling the house; it is about not buying it.
3. This is a **fact-finding** question. **C** is correct. You read *You can help me, Lou. We can keep watch and hide it from Mum and Dad* (see line 8). **A** is partly true because Steven wants Lou to hide the note; but it is incorrect because Steven wants Lou to keep watch and only hide it at a particular time—when the people coming to see the house have left. **B** is incorrect. Steven does not want Lou to say anything to Mum and Dad. The note is a secret.
4. This is a **fact-finding** question. **B** is correct. You read *I love living on this island* (see line 11). Steven and Lou live on an island. **A** and **C** are incorrect as they don't live in the city or in the suburbs.
5. This is a **fact-finding** question. **B** is correct. You read *We'll really get into trouble if Mum and Dad see it* (see line 10). **A** is incorrect because it isn't only Steven that Lou thinks will get into trouble. **C** is incorrect. The text does not state that Mum and Dad will understand.
6. This is a **fact-finding** question. You read the fact that Steven says *I love living on this island* (see line 11).

The visitor (page 12)

1 B	**2** C	**3** B	**4** A
5 A	**6** See below		

Explanations

1. This is a **fact-finding** question. **B** is correct. You read *Last year, at Christmas time, our family rented a holiday house* (see lines 2–3). **A** and **C** are incorrect because the text does not say that the holiday house was rented in the morning or yesterday.
2. This is a **fact-finding** question. **C** is correct. You read *There was a large area of bush beside the house* (see lines 4–5). **A** and **B** are incorrect because the house was not beside a hill or the sea. It was *on a hill near the sea* (see line 4).
3. This is a **fact-finding** question. **B** is correct. You read *It looked like a long, diamond-patterned rope* (see lines 9–10). **A** is incorrect. The snake didn't look like something on the driveway. It WAS something on the driveway. **C** is incorrect. The pattern looked like diamonds but the snake didn't look like diamonds.
4. This is a **fact-finding** question. **A** is correct. You read *It stretched from the bottom to the top of the driveway* (see lines 10–12). **B** is incorrect as the 'rope' did not stretch across the driveway. **C** is incorrect because the 'rope' did not stretch from the driveway to the house.
5. This is a **fact-finding** question. **A** is correct. You read *Dad told me to stay inside* (see line 14). **B** is incorrect because Dad did not say to stay at the window. **C** is incorrect because Dad did not say to stand on the driveway.

6 This is a **fact-finding** question. Dad said to leave the python alone so it could go back to the bush. He also said they would call Parks and Wildlife if the snake was still there the next day.

Brush turkey thinks it's a chicken (page 13)

1 C	**2** A	**3** C	**4** A
5 B	**6** See below		

Explanations

1 This is a **fact-finding** question. **C** is correct. You read '*We call it Bruce*' (see line 30). **A** is incorrect because Max is the boy being interviewed. **B** is incorrect because Sarah is the local reporter.

2 This is a **fact-finding** question. **A** is correct. You read '*When it was very small it … looked like a little duck.*' (see lines 9–13). **B** and **C** are incorrect because it looked like a duck and not a chicken or a baby turkey. It was a *baby brush turkey* (see lines 14–15), but Max says it *looked like a little duck* (see line 13).

3 This is a **fact-finding** question. **C** is correct. You read *Soon the baby brush turkey was living in the hen house* (see lines 14–16). **A** and **B** are incorrect because the baby brush turkey lives in the hen house, not the house or the garden.

4 This is a **fact-finding** question. **A** is correct. You read *the baby brush turkey pecked up its share* (see lines 18–19) of food. **B** and **C** are incorrect because the baby brush turkey didn't chew or gobble its food.

5 This is a **fact-finding** question. **B** is correct. You read *as it became an adult, the brush turkey's appearance changed completely* (see lines 23–26). **A** is incorrect because the brush turkey did not turn into a chicken. **C** is incorrect because the brush turkey learned to roost as a baby, not as an adult.

6 This is a **fact-finding** question. You read *the chickens think it* [the brush turkey] *is just another chicken* (see lines 27–29).

Our virtual tour (page 14)

1 B	**2** C	**3** B	**4** B
5 A	**6** See below		

Explanations

1 This is a **fact-finding** question. **B** is correct. You read *We clicked on a website for historic houses* (see lines 5–6). **A** is incorrect because houses is only part of the answer. The site is not for all houses, only historic houses. **C** is incorrect because virtual tours is not what the site was specifically for.

2 This is a **fact-finding** question. **C** is correct. You read *There was a guide who talked about the historic houses* (see lines 8–9). **A** and **B** are incorrect because neither a teacher nor a class member talked about the houses on the website.

3 This is a **fact-finding** question. **B** is correct. You read *Most of the houses were … built well over a hundred years ago* (see lines 9–11). **A** and **C** are incorrect because over a hundred years ago is neither in modern times nor a short time ago.

4 This is a **fact-finding** question. **B** is correct. You read *Most of the houses were big* (see lines 9–10). **A** is incorrect because 'old-fashioned' describes the kitchen equipment. **C** is incorrect because 'amazing' describes the gardens.

5 This is a **fact-finding** question. **A** is correct. You read *the beds looked much higher than the beds we have today* (see line 13). **B** and **C** are incorrect because these are not facts in the text.

6 This is a **fact-finding** question. You read that *some people needed the steps to climb into their beds!* (see lines 14–15)

Dugongs (page 15)

1 B	**2** C	**3** B	**4** B
5 C	**6** See below		

Explanations

1 This is a **fact-finding** question. **B** is correct. You read *they can remain under water for up to six minutes* (see lines 3–4). **A** and **C** are incorrect. These times they state are not facts in the text.

2 This is a **fact-finding** question. **C** is correct. You read *Dugongs eat the seagrass* (see line 7). **A** is incorrect as this is how dugongs eat and not what they eat. **B** is incorrect. This is not a fact in the text.

3 This is a **fact-finding** question. **B** is correct. You read *Most of the world's dugongs live off the coast of Australia* (see lines 5–6). **A** is incorrect because the question asks where dugongs are rather than what dugongs might be doing. **C** in incorrect. All dugongs live in sea water.

4 This is a **fact-finding** question. **B** is correct. You read that they *breathe air* (see line 3). **A** is incorrect as the text does not tell how dugongs find each other. **C** is incorrect because seagrass is on the seabed. Dugongs would not come to the surface to find it.

5 This is a **fact-finding** question. **C** is correct. You read *seagrass that grows in warm shallow sea water* (see lines 7–8). **A** is incorrect as it does not mention *sea*. **B** is incorrect because the text says seagrass grows where the water is shallow rather than anywhere in the sea. (Grass needs sunlight to grow.)

6 This is a **fact-finding** question. You read that dugongs mainly eat seagrass. When seagrass dies, dugongs starve. Seagrass dies when water gets polluted.

HELP WANTED (page 16)

1 B	**2** A	**3** C	**4** B
5 C	**6** See below		

Explanations

1 This is a **fact-finding** question. **B** is correct. You read *the terrible troll that lives under our Hartford Shire Bridge* (see lines 3–5). **A** is incorrect as the troll does not live on the bridge. **C** is incorrect. The troll does not live in a cave. The villagers want the troll hunter to take the troll to a cave.

2 This is a **fact-finding** question. **A** is correct. You read *The Village of Hartford needs help with the terrible troll* (see lines 3–4) and *We want it taken away* (see lines 8–9). **B** is incorrect. You read *We don't want to harm the troll* (see line 8). The villagers don't want the troll killed. **C** is incorrect. The troll does need to be captured but what the villagers want is for it to be taken away.

3 This is a **fact-finding** question. **C** is correct. You read *Our villagers are too frightened to use the bridge. The troll is eating our goats* (see lines 5–6). **A** is incorrect. The text does not say that villagers are being eaten. **B** is incorrect because it is not the full answer.

4 This is a **fact-finding** question. **B** is correct. You read *Applications for the job of Troll Hunter should be sent to: Post Office Manager, Hartford* (see lines 11–12). **A** and **C** are incorrect. These are not facts in the text.

5 This is a **fact-finding** question. **C** is correct. You read *We seek a brave person who will take the troll away* (see lines 7–8). **A** is incorrect. You don't need to be a Post Office Manager to apply for the job. **B** is incorrect. The poster says a *brave person* (see lines 7) is needed. It doesn't specify a man.

6 This is a **fact-finding** question. The answer is *a cave, far away* (see lines 9–10) from the village.

Invisibility potion (page 17)

1 A	**2** C	**3** B	**4** B
5 C	**6** See below		

Explanations

1 This is a **fact-finding** question. **A** is correct. You read *WARNING! Only use once a week or the effect becomes permanent* (see line 2). **B** is incorrect as this statement does not answer the question. **C** is incorrect as this is not a fact in the text.

2 This is a **fact-finding** question. **C** is correct. You read *This potion allows the user to become invisible for exactly 60 minutes* (see line 4). This means that after 60 minutes you will be visible again. **A** is incorrect. You become invisible instantly, rather than after 60 minutes. **B** is incorrect. If you took off your clothes you would remain naked but you would not become naked after 60 minutes.

3 This is a **fact-finding** question. **B** is correct. You read *Store in airtight container in refrigerator* (see line 16). **A** is incorrect as this is not a fact in the text. **C** is incorrect. The potion is rolled into balls. This is not where the balls are kept.

4 This is a **fact-finding** question. **B** is correct. You read *Chew and swallow 1 ball to become instantly invisible* (see lines 18–19). **A** is incorrect as you do not need to chew and swallow all the ingredients. **C** is incorrect. This answer tells how often to take the potion rather than how much to take.

5 This is a **fact-finding** question. **C** is correct. You read *clothing will not become invisible* (see line 5). If you want to be invisible you need to remove your clothes because people will see your clothes walking around. **A** is incorrect. This does not answer the question. **B** is incorrect. Although it might be true, it is not a fact in the text or the reason to take off your clothes.

6 This is a **fact-finding** question. You read *1 cup roasted rock lily stems* (see line 10). Roasting is a cooking process. The other ingredients are used raw.

Synthesis questions

Try gymnastics (page 20)

1 B	**2** C	**3** A	**4** C
5 C	**6** See below		

Explanations

1 This is a **synthesis** question. **B** is correct. Anna enjoys gymnastics and wants other children to try it. **A** is incorrect as the text is not a set of instructions. **C** is incorrect. The text tells why Anna likes gymnastics but not what it is.

2 This is a **synthesis** question. **C** is correct. The text has a list of all the reasons why Anna enjoys gymnastics. **A** and **B** are incorrect. These are facts in the text but not the main idea of the text.

3 This is a **synthesis** question. **A** is correct. Another reason Anna would like gymnastics is to improve her flexibility. This idea belongs in the list of reasons. **B** and **C** are incorrect. These are not reasons for doing gymnastics.

4 This is a **synthesis** question. **C** is correct. You read *It is good exercise. It makes me strong. It improves my balance and coordination* (see lines 6–8). The main reason that Anna recommends gymnastics is because she sees it as being such good exercise. **A** and **B** are incorrect. The fact that her brother does gymnastics and other children enjoy it are not included in Anna's list of reasons for recommending gymnastics.

5 This is a **synthesis** question. **C** is correct. The music is good but not essential to health. **A** and **B** are incorrect. They are both about fitness and therefore health.

6 This is a **synthesis** question. You read *I recommend gymnastics to other children* (see line 3). Then you read the conclusion, *I know other children would enjoy it just as my brother and I do* (see lines 14–15). You can work out that the audience for the text will be children, especially children Anna's age.

COME FRUIT-PICKING (page 21)

1 A	**2** B	**3** C	**4** B
5 4, 3, 2, 1	**6** See below		

Explanations

1 This is a **synthesis** question. **A** is correct. The website aims to persuade families to come fruit-picking at Fruit-pickers. **B** is incorrect. The website does invite people to join Friends of Fruit-pickers but this is not the main purpose of the website. **C** is incorrect. The website suggests that people pick a range of fruits, not only strawberries.

2 This is a **synthesis** question. **B** is correct. This information is about what you can do with the fruit after it is picked. You can eat it or take it home. **A** is incorrect as this part of the text introduces the reader to fruit-picking. **C** is incorrect because this part of the text is the introduction to the farm. Freezing the fruit belongs later in the order of events.

3 This is a **synthesis** question. **C** is correct. There is no information about the health benefits of fruit. **A** is incorrect as information about fruit-picking seasons is available when you click here. **B** is incorrect as information about where the orchards are is available when you type your postcode.

4 This is a **synthesis** question. **B** is correct. Connect ideas across the text to see that the main message is that the freshly picked fruit is delicious. Words such as *dripping with juice-licking goodness*; *delicious*; and *mouth-watering* (see lines 5–8) tell readers how delicious the fruit is to eat. **A** is incorrect. Although capitals are used for the word *FREE* (see line 3), this is only used once. **C** is incorrect. The text does not say that fruit-picking is hard work.

5 This is a **synthesis** question. The order the website suggests is **4** Take some fruit home. **3** Eat the fruit. **2** Pick the fruit. **1** Enter the farm.

6 This is a **synthesis** question. The text says *Click here for recipes* (see line 7). You would use your computer's mouse or your finger on a touch screen or a stylus to click on the link to open a new web page for the recipes.

Our experiment (page 22)

1 C	**2** B	**3** C	**4** A
5 yes	**6** See below		

Explanations

1 This is a **synthesis** question. **C** is correct. The text tells what happened in a science experiment. **A** is incorrect. The text is not a story. **B** is incorrect. The text does not give instructions. Instructions tell what to do. This text tells what happened.

2 This is a **synthesis** question. **B** is correct. You read the introduction, *My class did a fun experiment* (see line 2). Then you read *It looked good* (see line 9). You can tell that the writer enjoyed the experiment. You read *We learned that* (see line 10) and you can tell the writer thought the activity was useful and interesting. **A** is incorrect. The writer learned things so did not think it was a waste of time. **C** is incorrect. You can connect ideas to work out that the experiment worked well.

3 This is a **synthesis** question. **C** is correct. Connect the ideas across the text to work out that the green dye coloured the water so you could see the water and gas rise. **A** is incorrect. The text does not say that the dye made the bottle look pretty. **B** is incorrect because the dye did not colour the oil.

4 This is a **synthesis** question. **A** is correct. Work out where you might find a text like this by thinking about who might be interested in reading it. The text tells what happened in a classroom experiment. A school newsletter might publish a student's writing so that families can read about things students are doing at school. **B** and **C** are incorrect. A newspaper and a science book would not publish a student recount.

5 This is a **synthesis** question. The answer is yes. Connect ideas in paragraph three and the final paragraph to work out that any colour of food colouring would work. The colour makes no difference to what happens with gas, oil and water.

6 This is a **synthesis** question. Even though the child is having fun and looks interested the photo does not suit the text. The photo shows different equipment from that described in the text.

Book review (page 23)

1 B	**2** C	**3** B	**4** 3, 1, 2
5 C	**6** See below		

Explanations

1 This is a **synthesis** question. **B** is correct. The text tells about a book Jian has read. Jian tells readers what the book is about. **A** is incorrect. The text is not mainly about Peter and his father. The text only tells about Peter and his father as part of the story *The Treasure Box*. **C** is incorrect. The text is not mainly about a treasure. It tells about the treasure as part of Jian's review of the book.

2 This is a **synthesis** question. **C** is correct. Paragraph one tells you that the *city is bombed* (see line 5). Paragraph two tells you that Peter and his father *flee the city* (see line 7). Connect these two ideas to work out the answer. **A** is incorrect. It is a fact in the text but not the reason Peter and his father fled the city. **B** is incorrect as this is what Peter and his father did after they fled the city.

3 This is a **synthesis** question. **B** is correct. It is the only answer that makes sense. Readers of the book might wonder how Peter found the treasure. **A** and **C** are incorrect. They are already answered in the text. Readers are told that the book and words are the treasure (**A**). Readers are told that the treasure was safe at the end (**C**).

4 This is a **synthesis** question. 3, 1, 2 is the order of events in the story. The city was bombed; Peter promised to look after the treasure; Peter dug up the treasure.

5 This is a **synthesis** question. **C** is correct. Jian agrees with the characters in the story and thinks that books are treasure that everyone can share. **A** and **B** are incorrect because the main idea of *The Treasure Box* is not buried treasure or about Peter finding a treasure.

6 This is a **synthesis** question. Jian likes the idea that a book turns out to be the treasure and he also likes the illustrations in the book.

My hair (page 24)

1 A	**2** B	**3** B	**4** C
5 B	**6** See below		

Explanations

1 This is a **synthesis** question. **A** is correct. Katy thinks of many different ways she could change her hair. **B** is incorrect. Katy does think of having different colours in her hair but colour is only one of the changes she thinks about. **C** is incorrect. Katy only tells what her parents think in stanza 4.

2 This is a **synthesis** question. **B** is correct. You read *I'd like a different hair style, / Some stripes of pink or green* (see lines 2–3) at the beginning of the first stanza. **A** and **C** are incorrect because Katy thinks of growing her hair long or cutting it short later in the poem.

3 This is a **synthesis** question. **B** is correct. In stanza 2 Katy writes about how hard her hair is to manage or control. **A** is incorrect because she talks about colouring her hair in stanza 1. **C** is incorrect because she talks about cutting her hair in stanza 3.

4 This is a **synthesis** question. **C** is correct. The poem is about Katy trying to make up her mind about what to do with her hair. **A** is incorrect because Katy only thinks about cutting her hair in stanza 3. **B** is incorrect because Katy only thinks about a mohawk in stanza 4.

5 This is a **synthesis** question. **B** is correct. In stanza 4 Dad suggests a mohawk but Mum disagrees. **A** is incorrect. Katy has not decided what to do about her hair so her parents can't disagree with her. **C** is incorrect. This is not what the poem says in stanza 4.

6 This is a **synthesis** question. Connect ideas in the text to work out that Katy decides not to change her hair just yet because she can't make up her mind what to do with it.

Testing, testing (page 25)

1 B	**2** C	**3** B	**4** A
5 B	**6** See below		

Explanations

1 This is a **synthesis** question. **B** is correct. Basil wanted a princess for his wife but Ferdy wanted *a normal, easy-going girl* (see lines 2–3) for his wife. **A** is incorrect as there is no information about the types of mattress either prince likes. **C** is incorrect as there is no evidence about the types of food either prince likes.

2 This is a **synthesis** question. **C** is correct. The moral of the story is that you should make choices that suit you and not choices that suit others. **A** is incorrect because Basil was happy with his princess wife. **B** is incorrect because the story is not about eating apples to stay healthy and keep the doctor away.

3 This is a **synthesis** question. **B** is correct. Ferdy thinks up his own test by exchanging the three peas for larger fruits and vegetables under the mattresses. **A** is incorrect because Ferdy decides to marry his girlfriend after she passes his test. **C** is incorrect. Ferdy's girlfriend did sleep with fruits and vegetables under the mattresses but only after Ferdy had thought of this twist to Basil's test.

4 This is a **synthesis** question. **A** is correct. Ferdy's test proved that his girlfriend is easy going. She doesn't fuss when there are objects under her mattresses. **B** is incorrect because Ferdy's test is useful. It helps him find the kind of wife he wants. **C** is incorrect because Ferdy's test proves that his girlfriend is not a fussy princess like Basil's wife.

5 This is a **synthesis** question. **B** is correct. The text is a story. Its purpose is to entertain. **A** and **C** are incorrect. The purpose of the text is not to give instructions for a special test or to teach men how to find wives.

6 This is a **synthesis** question. You read *Prince Ferdy didn't want a princess for his wife. He wanted a normal, easy-going girl* (see lines 2–3). You might predict that the marriage would not have worked very well and Ferdy and his bride would have been unhappy.

Cockroaches (page 26)

1 B	**2** C	**3** B	**4** C
5 A	**6** See below		

Explanations

1 This is a **synthesis** question. **B** is correct. You read *Native cockroaches are good … And they do other things to help nature* (see lines 6–7). You can draw the conclusion that some people, like David, don't know that native cockroaches are good for the environment. **A** is incorrect. Introduced cockroaches are pests. **C** is incorrect because the text tells you that frogs eat cockroaches and native cockroaches don't eat frogs.

2 This is a **synthesis** question. **C** is correct. Selina defends native cockroaches when David says they are all disgusting. **A** is incorrect. This title does not suit the content of the text. When David says that all cockroaches are disgusting and that they all spread disease, Selina tells David that not all of them spread disease (see line 3). Most of the text is about native cockroaches being useful or important for the environment. **B** is incorrect. The food web is not the main focus of the text.

3 This is a **synthesis** question. **B** is correct. David gives an opinion. He is telling Selina what he thinks about cockroaches. **A** is incorrect. David is not starting an argument. **C** is incorrect. David is not describing cockroaches other than to say what he thinks of them.

4 This is a **synthesis** question. **C** is correct. The main idea in the text is that some cockroaches (native cockroaches) are useful and important in nature but cockroaches in the home spread disease. **A** is incorrect. Selina respects what native cockroaches do for nature. She only dislikes cockroaches in the home. **B** is incorrect. The text does not give any advice about ridding your home of cockroaches.

5 This is a **synthesis** question. **A** is correct. Both children dislike cockroaches in their homes. **B** is incorrect as Selina doesn't talk about cockroaches spreading diseases. **C** is incorrect. You read *'Really?' asked David. He wasn't convinced* (see line 5). David is not ready to agree with Selina that cockroaches are useful.

6 This is a **synthesis** question. In column 1 the answers are 1, 3 and 6. In column 2 the answers are 2, 4 and 5.

Sharks (page 27)

1 A	**2** B	**3** B	**4** B
5 C	**6** See below		

Explanations

1 This is a **synthesis** question. **A** is correct. The poem is about sharks being deadly killers. **B** and **C** are incorrect. The poet says sharks have sharp teeth and are sneaky but these are not the main messages of the poem.

2 This is a **synthesis** question. **B** is correct. The main message of the poem is that sharks are part of nature. You read that sharks are *Important in the web of life* (see line 20); that they belong *in the ocean* (see line 22); and that they are *At home— / roaming the seas* (see lines 23–24). **A** and **C** are incorrect. These statements might be true in the poem but they do not sum up its main message.

3 This is a **synthesis** question. **B** is correct. This photo shows the shark *gracefully gliding … At home— / roaming the seas* (see lines 17–24). **A** and **C** show the shark attacking prey so they suit Poem 1.

4 This is a **synthesis** question. **B** is correct. They are both about the same subject—sharks. **A** is incorrect because the poems are not about ocean animals in general. **C** is incorrect. The poems do not tell readers what they should think about sharks.

5 This is a **synthesis** question. **C** is correct. 'Impressive' is a word that could belong in both poems. The *Terrifying* (see line 13) shark in Poem 1 could be described as impressive. The *Magnificent* (see line 25) shark described in Poem 2 could also be called impressive. **A** and **B** are incorrect because these words could not belong in Poem 2.

6 This is a **synthesis** question. You might agree with the ideas in Poem 1 that sharks are cold-blooded monsters. The idea of a shark might frighten you. Or you might think that sharks are interesting or amazing and agree with the ideas in Poem 2.

Inferring questions

Peter has a feast (page 30)

1 B	**2** B	**3** A	**4** C
5 C	**6** See below		

Explanations

1 This is an **inferring** question. **B** is correct. You can work out that Mrs. Rabbit is talking to her four children—Flopsy, Mopsy, Cotton-tail and Peter. **A** and **C** are incorrect because Mrs. Rabbit's friends and neighbours are not in the story.

2 This is an **inferring** question. **B** is correct. You read *Your father had an accident there; he was put in a pie by Mrs. McGregor (see lines 4–5)*. You can work out that Mr. McGregor caught Mr Rabbit in his garden and Mrs. McGregor cooked him in a pie and they ate him. **A** and **C** are incorrect because there is no evidence that Mr. Rabbit ran away from the family or that he ate too much.

3 This is an **inferring** question. **A** is correct. Mrs. Rabbit fears her children will be caught and put in a pie. **B** is incorrect. There is no evidence that Mrs. Rabbit is afraid they will eat too much in Mr. McGregor's garden. **C** is incorrect. There is no evidence that Mrs. McGregor would want the rabbits for pets.

4 This is an **inferring** question. **C** is correct. You read *First he ate some lettuces and some French beans and then he ate some radishes and then, feeling rather sick (see lines 11–12)*. You can work out that he feels sick because he has eaten too much. **A** and **B** are incorrect as there is no evidence in the story that he has caught a germ or eaten a worm.

5 This is an **inferring** question. **C** is correct. Peter is feeling sick because he has eaten too much. See the *. You read *parsley* … *a herb that can help cure upset tummies (see lines 12–13)*. You can work out that Peter looks for some parsley to stop him feeling sick. **A** is incorrect. Peter is a greedy rabbit but he wants the parsley as a cure, not because he is still hungry. **B** is incorrect because the author doesn't tell us which herb Peter likes best.

6 This is an **inferring** question. Flopsy, Mopsy and Cotton-tail are said to be *good little bunnies (see lines 6–7)* because, unlike their brother, Peter, they did what their mother told them to do. You might also have noticed that the author says they gathered blackberries *(see lines 7–8)*. You can work out that they were taking the blackberries home to their mother. This is also different from Peter, who ate everything and did not gather anything to take home.

Wally the wombat (page 31)

1 A	**2** C	**3** B	**4** C
5 B	**6** See below		

Explanations

1 This is an **inferring** question. **A** is correct. You read *The stars twinkled as he waddled out (see line 5)*. You can work out that it is night-time in the story. **B** and **C** cannot be correct when the stars are out.

2 This is an **inferring** question. **C** is correct. Read between the lines to work out that Wally comes out of his burrow at night to eat. Wally is not eating in the morning (**A**). There is nothing in the text to suggest that he eats all day (**B**).

3 This is an **inferring** question. **B** is correct. You read *the fires could burn all the grass (see lines 13–14)*. You can read between the lines to work out that when bushfires burn all the grass Wally has nothing to eat. **A** is incorrect. The fact that bushfires come in the summertime is not what worried Wally about them. **C** is incorrect. The text says Wally is safe from bushfires in his deep burrow.

4 This is an **inferring** question. **C** is correct. At the beginning of the text Wally comes out of his burrow. The text ends with him thinking about the safety of his burrow. You can read between the lines to work out that he sleeps in his burrow. **A** and **B** are incorrect as there is nothing in the text to make you think that Wally sleeps on the sand mound that he walks past or in the grass.

5 This is an **inferring** question. **B** is correct. Wally sniffs as he exits his burrow and sniffs as he waddles to find the grasses. You read *His nose told him which way to go (see line 4)*. You can work out that he finds food using his sense of smell. **A** is incorrect. You read *He waddled past the sand mound he'd built with his strong claws (see lines 5–7)*. Wally uses strong claws for digging burrows, not for finding food. You can work out that he created the sand mound when he dug out his burrow. **C** is incorrect. There is nothing in the text to tell you that Wally uses his eyesight to look for food.

6 This is an **inferring** question. Wally eats grass. You read *he waddled on until he reached the native grass. He liked the black speargrass and the golden beard grass. He used his strong teeth to grind the leaves (see lines 10–12)*.

Big brother and little bother (page 32)

1 C	**2** B	**3** C	**4** See below
5 A	**6** See below		

Explanations

1 This is an **inferring** question. **C** is correct. You can infer that noise wakes the baby so Ben needs to keep quiet. **A** is incorrect. The text does not suggest that Ben always makes too much noise. **B** is incorrect. You should understand that Ben would not like to wake the baby.

2 This is an **inferring** question. **B** is correct. The monster picture that Ben uses to show his feelings has an annoyed expression on its face. It looks like it wants to scream and stomp its feet. The facial expression does not look worried (**A**) or sad (**C**).

3 This is an **inferring** question. **C** is correct. You can read between the lines to work out that when Mum sees the angry expression on Ben's face, she sends him to his room to calm down. You read *She says to go in my room and chill out (see line 9)*. **A** is incorrect because the text does not suggest that Mum is angry with Charlie. **B** is incorrect. You can work out that Mum is often busy with Charlie but this is not why she sends Ben to his room.

4 This is an **inferring** question. Charlie is a bother sometimes just because he is a baby and babies can't help crying, sleeping or needing attention.

5 This is an **inferring** question. **A** is correct. You can read between the lines and work out that Ben is a little jealous of the baby. **B** is incorrect. There is nothing in the text to tell readers that Ben needs help with homework. **C** is incorrect. There is nothing in the text to suggest that Ben wants to be the baby again. He says, *I like being the big brother* (see lines 10–11).

6 This is an **inferring** question. You should read between the lines and use your own knowledge about babies to work out the answer. Mum can't always stop Charlie from crying just because Ben has asked her to. You should work out that Mum might also find it upsetting if the baby cries loudly.

Should there be a set bedtime for seven- and eight-year-olds? (page 33)

1 B	2 A	3 A	4 A
5 B	6 See below		

Explanations

1 This is an **inferring** question. **B** is correct. Toby is the only child to argue that children should not have a set bedtime. **A** is incorrect. Anh says having a set bedtime is a help. **C** is incorrect. Hannah hates having a set bedtime but says she needs one.

2 This is an **inferring** question. **A** is correct. Anh says *Having a set bedtime is a real help* (see line 9). **B** is incorrect. You can work out that Jordan agrees with Hannah that he needs a set bedtime but he doesn't always like having one. **C** is incorrect because Anh says she does like having a set bedtime.

3 This is an **inferring** question. **A** is correct. Anh and Jordan call out *Yes!* (see line 14) after Hannah suggests bending the rules. This shows that the idea is popular with the three children. **B** is incorrect because this idea is the opposite of what is popular with the children. **C** is incorrect. This idea is only popular with one of the children, Toby.

4 This is an **inferring** question. **A** is correct. The only reason the children approve of a set bedtime is because it helps them wake up for school. **B** is incorrect. This reason doesn't make sense. **C** is incorrect. This reason is not suggested by any of the children.

5 This is an **inferring** question. **B** is correct. Hannah says *I hate having it!* (i.e. a set bedtime) (see line 6), whereas Jordan says he doesn't like having a set bedtime when he is watching something on TV. You can work out that they both accept the idea of having a set bedtime but Hannah likes it less than Jordan. **A** is incorrect. It is the opposite of Hannah's and Jordan's opinions. **C** is incorrect because their opinions are similar but not exactly the same.

6 This is an **inferring** question. The children call out *Yes!* (see line 14) because they like the idea of bending the rules to stay up late sometimes. Toby does not agree with bedtime rules so he does not join the other children to call out *Yes!* You read ***Toby:*** *I don't think children should have any set bedtime. It's healthier to go to sleep when you're tired* (see lines 3–4).

The trumpet player (page 34)

1 A	2 C	3 C	4 B
5 A	6 See below		

Explanations

1 This is an **inferring** question. **A** is correct. Amy's words *This was my chance* (see line 6) show that she is looking forward to something. You can read between the lines that she feels both nervous and excited. **B** is incorrect. Amy's heart would not somersault if she was feeling calm. **C** is incorrect. Amy is thinking about the chance her trumpet playing will give her. She is expecting this moment and is not surprised or unhappy about it.

2 This is an **inferring** question. **C** is correct. As soon as Amy hears it is time for her to play, her mind is on that. She barely notices anything else. **A** is incorrect. There is no evidence that Amy needs new glasses. **B** is incorrect. The girls may have been being friendly. This is not the reason Amy barely notices their actions.

3 This is an **inferring** question. **C** is correct. Susie and Evie are in class with Amy. **A** is incorrect because neither Susie's nor Evie's actions are those you would expect teachers to do. Also the teachers in the text are called by their proper titles: Ms Brown and Ms Scott. **B** is incorrect because there is no evidence that the girls are Amy's sisters.

4 This is an **inferring** question. **B** is correct. Amy needs a deep breath to begin playing her trumpet. **A** and **C** are incorrect. There is no evidence that Amy feels dizzy or that taking a deep breath is a bad habit she can't stop.

5 This is an **inferring** question. **A** is correct. Ms Brown's words show that she thinks Amy's playing has become much better. **B** is incorrect because this is the opposite of what Ms Brown's words suggest. **C** is incorrect. Ms Brown is not suggesting that Amy will never improve her playing in the future.

6 This is an **inferring** question. Amy's dream was to be chosen to play her trumpet at the eisteddfod.

Whose house is it anyway? (page 35)

1 A	2 B	3 C
4 B	5 See below	6 See below

Explanations

1 This is an **inferring** question. **A** is correct. Read between the lines. You can work out that what looks like a tall, hairy giant to the mouse is a human being—a man. **B** and **C** are incorrect because the giant the mouse sees is not a mouse of any kind.

2 This is an **inferring** question. **B** is correct. Read between the lines. You read *I'm just a tiny mouse* (see line 4) and He's *metres tall* (see line 5). From the mouse's point of view the human is scary because he is so huge. **A** is incorrect as there is no evidence that the giant has large teeth. **C** is incorrect. Shyness is not the reason the mouse is scared. Most things as tiny as a mouse would be scared of a human.

3 This is an **inferring** question. **C** is correct. Read between the lines. The giant has cooked the food and he is telling his family that it is time to come and eat. **A** and **B** are incorrect because there is no evidence in the text that a mouse trap has been set or that anyone is going to have a bath.

4 This is an **inferring** question. **B** is correct. Read between the lines. You work out that *in-betweens* (see line 9) look shorter than the giant to the mouse. In fact they are shorter members of the family who live in the house—probably the giant's wife and children. **A** is incorrect. The figures look like giants to the mouse but they are not mice. **C** is incorrect. Some of the *in-betweens* might include teenagers but there is nothing to say they are all teenagers.

5 This is an **inferring** question. Read between the lines. You work out that the chomping noise the mouse hears comes from the humans eating their meal. To the mouse's ears these *chomping, chomping* (see line 10) noises are loud and threatening.

6 This is an **inferring question**. Read between the lines. Mrs Mouse thinks living in a house with these giants is both frightening and dangerous. They are huge, scary creatures who make noisy, threatening *chomping* (see line 10) noises. Mrs Mouse thinks her own and her husband's lives could be in danger. Perhaps she thinks they could be next on the menu!

Mia's mistake (page 36)

1 C	2 C	3 A	4 C
5 B	6 See below		

Explanations

1 This is an **inferring** question. **C** is correct. You read *Not again, thought Mia. Please, no. I can't lose another one* (see line 4). You can work out that Mia had lost a school bag before. **A** is incorrect. You read *On the other side of the park a boy she didn't know had picked up her school bag* (see line 3). You can work out that this boy had not taken Mia's school bag before. **B** is incorrect. It relates to the boy rather than to what Mia was thinking.

2 This is an **inferring** question. **C** is correct. You read *Mia was starting to panic* (see line 6) and *Mia was going to be in trouble when her mother arrived* (see lines 7–8). You can work out that Mia wants to avoid getting into trouble with her mum. **A** is incorrect. There is nothing in the text to suggest that Mia wants to start a fight. Mia does not seem angry. She is just worried. **B** is incorrect. There is nothing in the text to suggest that Mia wants to make friends with the boy.

3 This is an **inferring** question. **A** is correct. You can work out that if Mia is not ready and waiting for her mum it makes her mum late for work. You read *But she wasn't allowed to leave the park. Not after last time. She had to be there when Mum arrived at 4 o'clock. Mum hated being late for work* (see lines 8–10). **B** and **C** are incorrect. There is nothing in the text to infer that Mia has to stay in the park because her mum worries she will get lost or run over by a car.

4 This is an **inferring** question. **C** is correct. You read *But Mia had to get her bag back. She started to run* (see lines 10–11). You can work out that Mia will chase the boy. **A** is incorrect. You can tell that Mia decides it's more important to get her bag back than to wait for her mum. **B** is incorrect. Mia *started to run* (see line 11). She doesn't start yelling again. There is no point in yelling. The boy had not heard her yelling before.

5 This is an **inferring** question. **B** is correct. You read that the boy has picked up Mia's school bag and that Mia's mother will be collecting her at the park at 4 pm. You can infer that the events occurred after school and not before school (**A**) or on the weekend (**C**).

6 This is an **inferring** question. The title of the text could mean a number of things. Mia's mistake might be that she left her bag on the other side of the park or that she followed the boy across the road against her mother's rule. Or perhaps Mia's mistake is that the boy did not have her bag at all. You can tell by the photo that Mia has a very common-looking bag. Many children probably have bags that look like this, especially from across a park. Mia's bag might still be where she had left it.

The invitation (page 37)

1 C	2 A	3 A
4 C	5 See below	6 See below

Explanations

1 This is an **inferring** question. **C** is correct. Read between the lines. Wolfie says that people have said he has sharp teeth and sharp claws. You can work out that this means people think he is dangerous. **A** is incorrect. There is nothing in the text to suggest that people have said the wolf is handsome. **B** is incorrect. It is not people who say the wolf is friendly; it is the wolf who says this about himself.

2 This is an **inferring** question. **A** is correct. Read between the lines. Wolfie denies that girls in red hoods are his favourite food so that the girl will think he won't want to eat her. He adds it to persuade the girl that she is safe to visit him. **B** is incorrect because this is the opposite of what Wolfie wants the girl to believe. **C** is incorrect. Wolfie did not want to frighten the girl.

3 This is an **inferring** question. **A** is correct. Read between the lines and use your own knowledge of fairytales. It is well known that if a wolf tries to lure you to its den, it should not be trusted. You can work out from this and the way the wolf protests he is harmless in his letter that he is a tricky character. You should work out that his invitation to dinner sounds like a trap. **B** and **C** are incorrect. The wolf may be proud of his home and may like to cook but these are not the reasons for his invitation.

4 This is an **inferring** question. **C** is correct. Read between the lines. In the second text the narrator says that when the girl went to the wolf's den *he had her for dinner* (see lines 21–22). In a different context *he had her for dinner* could mean that she went to his home and had dinner with him. In this text you can work out it means that the wolf ate the girl for his dinner. **A** and **B** are incorrect because what the narrator tells the reader (see line 25) shows that these things did not happen.

5 This is an **inferring** question. *The girl … believed the wolf* (see lines 20–21) means that the girl believed him (the wolf) when he said he wasn't a danger to her. She thought he was telling the truth when he offered her friendship.

6 This is an **inferring** question. Wolves in folktales are not to be trusted. It doesn't matter that he writes nice letters. It doesn't matter that he makes promises. It is important to remember that he is a wolf and so will behave like a wolf.

Language questions

Moving house (page 40)

1 B	**2** C	**3** B	**4** A
5 A	**6** See below		

Explanations

1 This is a **language** question. **B** is correct. The word *in* (see line 8) means that the racquet is in the boxes with the bat and skates. **A** is incorrect because the house is not the place where the racquet has been packed. **C** is incorrect because the racquet has been packed; it is not in the way.

2 This is a **language** question. **C** is correct. Gretchen is thinking only about packing when suddenly she remembers she has to leave her mates behind. **A** and **B** are incorrect because Gretchen's *Oh!* (see line 8) does not suggest that she feels frightened or happy.

3 This is a **language** question. **B** is correct. Mum is saying that Gretchen will be all right and that missing the tree will not be a problem. **A** is incorrect. Gretchen's mum is not referring to her own worries. **C** is incorrect because Gretchen's mum is talking about how Gretchen feels, not how Gretchen makes her feel.

4 This is a **language** question. **A** is correct. The word *you* in *Boxes—you guessed* (see line 24) speaks directly to the reader. **B** and **C** are incorrect because the reader is not spoken to directly in these lines.

5 This is a **language** question. **A** is correct. Gretchen feels that the packing will never end and it is taking forever. **B** is incorrect because Gretchen feels the opposite—moving house is slow and not quick. **C** is incorrect because there is no evidence that Gretchen doesn't want to move.

6 This is a **language** question. Gretchen feels that the packing will never end. Repeating the stanza about boxes being here, there and everywhere creates this feeling. It is as if time passes but the packing doesn't seem to get done. (Part of the reason for this is suggested in the illustration.) It is also common in poems and songs to repeat stanzas.

Apricot balls (page 41)

1 C	**2** C	**3** B	**4** B
5 A	**6** See below		

Explanations

1 This is a **language** question. **C** is correct. You read *This recipe is good for snacks. It is also a healthy lunch-box treat* (see lines 2–3). You can work out that *also* means that you can eat the apricot rolls as snacks AND as part of lunch. **A** and **B** might be true but this is not how *also* is used in the text.

2 This is a **language** question. **C** is correct. You read that the apricot rolls are not *suitable* (see line 19) for people with certain allergies. You can work out that the rolls might make them sick so they should not be eaten. **A** and **B** are incorrect. Not useful and not tasty are not the same as not to be eaten.

3 This is a **language** question. **B** is correct. You read that *honey* (see line 10) is an ingredient so you can work out that the apricot rolls are sweet. None of the ingredients are sour (**A**) or salty (**C**).

4 This is a **language** question. **B** is correct. You read *Store in fridge* (see line 16). This means to keep the apricot rolls in the fridge. **A** is incorrect as you are not told to go to a store or shop. **C** is incorrect as you would not eat the rolls in the fridge.

5 This is a **language** question. **A** is correct. You can work out that the *Method* (see line 12) tells you the steps to follow, in sequence, to make apricot rolls. **B** and **C** are incorrect. They tell you about the ingredients but not what to do with them as steps to follow.

6 This is a **language** question. *Dried* and *desiccated* are the correct answers. The recipe uses *dried apricots* and *desiccated coconut* (see lines 5–6). These fruits have had moisture taken out to help preserve them.

Litter report (page 42)

1 A	**2** B	**3** C	**4** B
5 C	**6** See below		

Explanations

1 This is a **language** question. **A** is correct. You can tell that CJ is excited about what has happened by the exclamation *Guess what!* (see line 4). CJ has news for Nana. **B** is incorrect because the exclamation is not a question. **C** is incorrect. CJ is not talking on the phone. CJ has typed an email.

2 This is a **language** question. **B** is correct. CJ is talking about something that happened to him or her and Dad. **A** is incorrect. CJ is writing to Nana. **C** is incorrect. The pronoun *we* includes the writer and one or more other person.

3 This is a **language** question. **C** is correct. The 'wrongdoer' is the litterer—the person doing the wrong thing. **A** is incorrect as the car owner may or may not have been in the car at the time. **B** is incorrect as the reporter is CJ's dad.

4 This is a **language** question. **B** is correct. The word *duty* (see line 9) in the text means 'responsibility', 'job' or 'role'. It does not mean 'business' (**A**) or 'purpose' (**C**).

5 This is a **language** question. **C** is correct. CJ will look out for litterers using his or her own eyes. There is nothing in the text to say that CJ is going to use binoculars (**A**). **B** is incorrect. CJ took a photo once the litterer was spotted. The camera recorded the evidence. It was not used to look for litterers.

6 This is a **language** question. The answer is that CJ took a photo of the car and its number plate. You know this when you read *Dad said, 'Quick! Take a photo of the car. Make sure you get the number plate.' So I did* (see lines 6–7).

At the museum (page 43)

1 C	**2** B	**3** A	**4** B
5 A	**6** See below		

Explanations

1 This is a **language** question. **C** is correct. Inquiries are questions. You visit the Inquiries area to ask questions about the museum. Examine the map and notice that the entrance leads visitors straight to Inquiries. **A** is incorrect because the Staff room is just for museum staff. Notice that this section of the museum is out of the way of visitors. **B**

is incorrect because the Learning centre is where visitors would go for activities.

2 This is a **language** question. **B** is correct. You can see that the Dolls area is placed between Musical instruments and Cars. **A** and **C** are incorrect because Dolls are not above or underneath the other displays.

3 This is a **language** question. **A** is correct. Storage means where things are stored. This is where things not on display would be kept in the museum. **B** is incorrect because the Kitchen is where cooking is done for the Cafe. **C** is incorrect because the Reading room is where visitors to the museum can read.

4 This is a **language** question. **B** is correct. The word *Manager* means the person in charge of a workplace. **A** and **C** are incorrect because you would not expect to find the office of the person in charge in the Gift shop or in the Staff room.

5 This is a **language** question. **A** is correct. You need to turn left at the Entrance hall and walk past the toilets to get to the Learning centre. **B** is incorrect because if you turn right and go through the 19th century toy display you can't get into the Learning centre. You should see on the diagram that the way is blocked from there. **C** is incorrect as that would take you outside the museum.

6 This is a **language** question. The skull of an ancient diprotodon is a fossil. The room that displays fossils is where you would find a skull. The word 'ancient' in the question is another clue because fossils are very old. You don't have to know the meaning of the word *diprotodon* to work out this answer. (A diprotodon is an ancient marsupial that is now extinct.)

Things to do when I'm bored (page 44)

1 A	**2** C	**3** A	**4** B
5 B	**6** See below		

Explanations

1 This is a **language** question. **A** is correct. Both 1 and 4 include names of people close to Alex. You read that Billy is Alex's little brother and Ichiro is Alex's friend. **B** and **C** are incorrect. 2, 6, 11, and 12 do not include any personal details.

2 This is a **language** question. **C** is correct. Riddles is the odd one out. Riddles are cleverly worded questions that are jokes. **A** and **B** are incorrect. You can classify or group the coins and stones as objects you can touch.

3 This is a **language** question. **A** is correct. You can work out that Alex uses the brackets to single out broccoli from other vegetables because Alex doesn't want it in the garden. **B** is incorrect. It would not be singled out with the word *not* in front of it if Alex liked broccoli and wanted it in the garden. **C** is incorrect. The brackets do not suggest that broccoli is not a vegetable.

4 This is a **language** question. **B** is correct. Thinking about pleasing Billy (1) and washing Nan's car (7) shows that Alex thinks of other people's needs. **A** is incorrect. Making a diorama (6) and taking better photographs (9) are not ways to help other people. **C** is incorrect. Making a vegetable garden (10) and setting up a treasure hunt (12) could be ways to help others but they are not worded in a way that shows this is Alex's plan.

5 This is a **language** question. **B** is correct. The brackets enclose the names of two hobbies Alex is thinking about as possible. **A** is incorrect because Alex is not thinking only of astronomy. **C** is incorrect because the bracketed words are not about whether a hobby is a good idea.

6 This is a **language** question. Answers will vary. The choice of activity should be supported with a reason.

Disappointment (page 45)

1 C	**2** C	**3** A	**4** B
5 B	**6** See below		

Explanations

1 This is a **language** question. **C** is correct. Ava says *I know* after her father says *Cheer up. You did your best. That's what counts* (see lines 2–3). You can work out when Ava says *I know* that she is agreeing with her father that she did do her best and that she does know doing your best is what counts. **A** is true but this information comes later in the text. **B** is an opinion that Ava has about her own performance but it is not what she refers to when she says *I know*.

2 This is a **language** question. **C** is correct. Dad says *You did your best. That's what counts* (see line 2). You can work out that he means that doing your best is what matters. **A** is incorrect because Dad does not say that success is what counts. **B** is incorrect because *counts* in the text is nothing to do with maths or adding up.

3 This is a **language** question. **A** is correct. You read that Dad says *Don't lose sight of why you go* (see line 12). He means that Ava shouldn't forget the reason she likes Little Athletics—because it's fun. **B** is incorrect. *Don't lose sight* is an expression. It does not really mean 'Don't go blind'. **C** is incorrect. *Don't lose sight* is not about worrying. It's about remembering or thinking about the reason for going to Little Athletics.

4 This is a **language** question. **B** is correct. *It's no use crying over spilt milk* (see line 15) is an expression that's used when someone makes a mistake that they can't undo. If you think about spilt milk you know you can't put milk back in its container once it's spilt. The expression means 'Don't waste time being upset because you can't change what has happened'. It does not actually have anything to do with milk (**A**). **C** is incorrect. The expression doesn't mean 'Don't cry at all when you are upset'.

5 This is a **language** question. **B** is correct. Dad says *You go* [to Little Athletics] *to have fun first and foremost* (see line 12). This means that having fun is the first and most important reason. **A** and **C** are not the meanings of *foremost* in the text.

6 This is a **language** question. Disappointment means feeling upset or sad or disheartened. You can work out that the title is *Disappointment* because Ava is disappointed in herself for not doing better.

The hare and the tortoise (page 46)

1 A	**2** C	**3** B
4 A	**5** See below	**6** See below

Explanations

1 This is a **language** question. **A** is correct. The word *steady* (see line 5) in the text means that the tortoise walked at the same even pace for the whole race. He didn't race ahead and then stop altogether, like the hare. **B** is incorrect. The tortoise was slow but this is not the meaning of *steady*. **C** is

incorrect. The tortoise *plodded on (see line 8)* but this is not the meaning of *steady*.

2 This is a **language** question. **C** is correct. You can tell that the hare is determined to win. You read his statements. He says *I am … I can … I will … I will … (see lines 3–4)* **A** is incorrect. The hare was not angry when he said *I will win! (see line 4)*. **B** is incorrect. The hare might have been surprised after the tortoise had won the race. The hare was not surprised before the start of the race.

3 This is a **language** question. **B** is correct. The tortoise was calm. You read that the tortoise was as still as a statue *(see line 5)* before the race. **A** and **C** are incorrect. The hare is the one who is excited and boastful, not the tortoise.

4 This is a **language** question. **A** is correct. The hare is feeling energetic before the race. He is hopping on the spot *(see line 3)*. **B** is incorrect. The hare went to sleep during the race. **C** is incorrect. The hare probably felt foolish for boasting he could win and then letting the tortoise win. But that was after the race, not before the race.

5 This is a **language** question. You need to consider what the character of the tortoise might be thinking at this particular time in the story. Your answer could be 'I'm glad that hare has gone to sleep' or 'That silly hare is sleeping'.

6 This is a **language** question. *Slow and steady wins the race (see line 10)* is the moral of the fable. It means that you should work steadily to reach your goal. Working too hard for a little while and then doing nothing is not the best way to reach your goal.

Grandad (page 47)

1 A	**2** B	**3** C
4 B	**5** a chariot	**6** See below

Explanations

1 This is a **language** question. **A** is correct. Work out the meaning of *inappropriate* by thinking about how it is used in the text. You read *he's not allowed to bring it to the dinner table. Dad says that would be inappropriate (see lines 3–5)*. You can work out that Dad thinks it would be unacceptable to have fart sounds while the family is eating. The prefix *in-* means 'not'. *Inappropriate* means 'not appropriate'. This is the opposite of suitable (**B**). You can work out that Dad would not think the fart cushion funny (**C**) at the dinner table.

2 This is a **language** question. **B** is correct. You read *Grandad has bristly white eyebrows (see line 6)*. You can work out that bristly means 'prickly' rather than 'soft' (**A**). **C** is a colour so does not answer a question about what the eyebrows feel like.

3 This is a **language** question. **C** is correct. To watch something *like a hawk (see line 11)* means to watch it carefully. Hawks have very good eyesight. **A** and **B** don't make sense in the text because the writer needs to watch her cheating grandad carefully, rather than with beady eyes (**A**) or from up in the air (**B**).

4 This is a **language** question. **B** is correct. You read *When he offers me a ride he says, 'M'lady, your chariot awaits' (see lines 12–13)*. You can work out that the writer is a girl because Grandad calls her *M'lady*. 'My Lady' is a formal term used to address a female respectfully. It is an old-fashioned term. **A** is incorrect as a grandson is a boy or male. **C** is incorrect. The text tells about Grandad but is not written by Grandad.

5 This is a **language** question. You can work out the answer when you read *He rides a motor scooter to the shops. When he offers me a ride he says, 'M'lady, your chariot awaits' (see lines 12–13)*. Grandad calls his motor scooter a *chariot*. A chariot was a horse-drawn carriage used long before cars were invented. Grandad is making a joke, referring to things from the olden days.

6 This is a **language** question. The statement means that the writer is comparing Grandad to a walrus. Grandad has bristly eyebrows, a moustache and a bald head so he might look like a walrus. The writer also might think Grandad's whiskers would feel like a walrus's whiskers.

Judgement questions

Nicki's problem (page 50)

1 C	**2** C	**3** A
4 A	**5** See below	**6** See below

Explanations

1 This is a **judgement** question. **C** is correct. You can judge that Nicki thinks she made a mistake but she is thinking about a way to fix it. **A** is incorrect. Nicki thinks about her mother. She saved $20 for the gift. She is now trying to think of a solution to the fact that she has no money for a gift. **B** is incorrect. There is no evidence in the text to support a judgement that Nicki is jealous of Rachel.

2 This is a **judgement** question. **C** is correct. You can judge that Nicki mainly feels sad because she has no gift for her mother's birthday. You can judge that **A** is incorrect. Look at Nicki's facial expression in the photo. Nicki does not feel cheerful. **B** is incorrect. Nicki is upset with herself rather than angry.

3 This is a **judgement** question. **A** is correct. You can judge that Nicki would have chosen not to spend all her money. **B** and **C** are incorrect. Just because she stayed at her dad's and went to the shopping centre with Rachel does not mean she had to spend all her money. She still could have done these things.

4 This is a **judgement** question. **A** is correct. You can judge that Rachel's mother (Nicki's stepmother) is not mean to Nicky. She took both girls to the shopping centre. She has Nicky to stay on some weekends. **B** and **C** are likely to be true based on evidence in the text. You could make a judgement that Nicki and Rachel enjoy doing things together. You could also make a judgement that Nicki's father enjoys having her to stay with him.

5 This is a **judgement** question. You can make a judgement about Nicki's mother based on the story and on your experience of mothers and adult relatives. You should judge that Nicki's mother would not expect Nicki to buy her a gift. You might suggest that she'd rather Nicki make her something or did something special for her.

6 This is a **judgement** question. You can judge that if you were Nicki you would think of something to do for your mother on her birthday that did not cost any money. For example, Nicky could make a gift and a

card. She could promise to be more helpful around the house. She could prepare breakfast for her mum or write a pledge to do the dishes for a month. You might suggest that Nicky could borrow money from her father but this solution is unlikely. You can judge that her father did not give her money to spend when she stayed at his place.

World Ranger Day (page 51)

1 C	**2** B	**3** B
4 A	**5** See below	**6** See below

Explanations

1. This is a **judgement** question. **C** is correct. You read *This special day makes people think about the important jobs that rangers do (see lines 2–3).* You can judge that Cathy thinks the job of a ranger is important. **A** is incorrect. You read that Cathy's mum was excited to watch the female turtle lay eggs. You would not judge this to be boring. **B** is incorrect. Cathy doesn't make her mother's job sound like hard work.
2. This is a **judgement** question. **B** is correct. You can judge that Cathy is inspired by her mum and wants to be like her. **A** is incorrect. Paragraph one tells you that some rangers in some countries do dangerous jobs but you can judge that Cathy is not worried about her mum's safety helping turtles. **C** is incorrect. Even though Cathy would like to do her mum's job one day you can judge that she is not jealous of her mum.
3. This is a **judgement** question. **B** is correct. You can judge that Cathy wants readers to feel that rangers like her mum are looking after the turtles so turtles are in safe hands. **A** is incorrect. Even though Cathy tells readers about problems faced by hatchlings you can judge that Cathy does not seem worried about the turtles' future. **C** is incorrect. Cathy's mother was excited to watch the female lay her eggs but you should judge that this is not the most important idea in the text.
4. This is a **judgement** question. **A** is correct. Cathy is proud of Sea Country. She refers to it as *our Sea Country (see line 5).* This is evidence that she wants to protect it as her mother does. **B** and **C** are not true based on the evidence in the text.
5. This is a **judgement** question. You can judge that hatchlings need help because they face many dangers. You read that they can drown in their nests. You can judge that land predators might eat them before they make it into the water. You read that they can get run over by four-wheel-drive vehicles. You might also think that if hatchlings fail to survive to become adults and breed, then turtle numbers will decline. You can judge that they need help to survive the dangers they face as hatchlings.
6. This is a **judgement** question. You have to judge for yourself whether the ideas in the text make you think you'd want to be a ranger. The information in the text can help you judge that the work of a ranger is important, fun and interesting. You could also decide that you would not like to be a ranger. You must give reasons to explain your judgement.

Pets (page 52)

1 B	**2** A	**3** C
4 C	**5** See below	**6** See below

Explanations

1. This is a **judgement** question. **B** is correct. You read all the jobs Vivienne does and you can judge that she is a responsible pet owner. **A** and **C** are incorrect. You can tell by the photo that Vivienne adores Harry but there is no evidence in the text to say she complains about her jobs or tries to get out of doing them.
2. This is a **judgement** question. **A** is correct. You can judge that Harry is a sociable and energetic dog when you read *he loves to run off leash with his friends from the neighbourhood (see lines 4–5).* **B** is incorrect. There is nothing in the text that says that he is a good guard dog. **C** is incorrect. You can judge that he is clean when Vivienne and her mum bathe him but you can judge that he is not lazy because he loves to run with other dogs.
3. This is a **judgement** question. **C** is correct. It is the answer that makes sense. You can judge that Harry likes to run. **A** is incorrect. You should judge that an energetic dog would be likely to want to stay in the park longer. **B** is incorrect. It is unlikely that Harry would be worried about bath time at this moment in the park. Worrying about things that might happen in the future is something humans do. It is not something that an animal is likely to do except in a story.
4. This is a **judgement** question. **C** is correct. You can judge that Molly does what she wants in Will's home. She sits where she likes and sleeps where she likes. She has trained Will to give her attention when she wants it and to leave her in peace when she signals that she wants to be left alone. You should judge that Molly thinks that Will is an obedient human. **A** is incorrect. The evidence in the text suggests that Will does what Molly likes him to do. **B** is incorrect. You should judge that only a cartoon cat or a storybook cat would think about its owner's homework in this way. A real pet cat is not going to be checking up on homework.
5. This is a **judgement** question. You should judge that Molly would be more suited to a home unit than a dog, provided pets are allowed in the unit block. Molly does not need to be exercised or bathed so she would be easier for an elderly person to manage. You might also judge that neither pet would be suitable because they both require an amount of work.
6. This is a **judgement** question. Your choice will depend on whether you prefer the energetic Harry or the sleepy Molly. Your choice will also depend on your past or current experience of cats and dogs as pets; what your family preference is; the size and type of pet appropriate for where you live; and how much time your family has to exercise a dog or care for a pet.

Chinese New Year (page 53)

1 B	2 A	3 A	4 C
5 C	6 See below		

Explanations

1 This is a **judgement** question. **B** is correct. Mary Jo's father asks her if she would like to accept the invitation. You can judge that he allows her to decide for herself. **A** is incorrect. Mary Jo's father does not tell her that she must accept the invitation. **C** is incorrect. Mary Jo's father does not say he would rather Mary Jo stay at home and refuse the invitation.

2 This is a **judgement** question. **A** is correct. You read that Mary Jo says *Well, I hope I'll know what to do (see line 6)*. You judge that this means she is nervous about doing the wrong thing as she isn't sure how to follow Chinese customs. **B** is incorrect. Her words refer to when she is at Chinese New Year celebrations, not how to reply to the invitation. **C** is incorrect. Mary Jo is worried about accepting the invitation but there is no evidence that she doesn't want to accept it.

3 This is a **judgement** question. **A** is correct. You judge that Chen is proud of her Chinese background. She shares Chinese customs with Mary Jo by showing her how to use chopsticks. She helps Mary Jo enjoy the Chinese New Year celebrations with her family. **B** is incorrect. There is no evidence of Chen being worried about her Chinese background. **C** is incorrect. Chen already knows about Chinese customs.

4 This is a **judgement** question. **C** is correct. Mary Jo talks to her father about her private worries. You judge that this makes their relationship trusting. **A** and **B** are incorrect as there are no signs of Mary Jo's relationship with her father being unhappy or unfriendly.

5 This is a **judgement** question. **C** is correct. You can judge that Mary Jo feels excited and happy at the end of the night. The way she describes the events at the Chinese New Year celebrations shows readers how much she enjoyed them and what fun she had. **A** is incorrect. Mary Jo was a bit worried about going to the Chinese New Year celebrations but they did not frighten or worry her when she was there. **B** is incorrect. There is no evidence to suggest that Mary Jo is jealous or annoyed.

6 This is a **judgement** question. Mary Jo learned that she can try new experiences and not worry so much beforehand.

A Dreaming story: Tiddalik (page 54)

1 B	2 B	3 B	4 C
5 B	6 See below		

Explanations

1 This is a **judgement** question. **B** is correct. You judge that Tiddalik's actions show he thinks only of his own thirst and he drinks the water greedily. He doesn't think of anyone else's needs. **A** is incorrect because there is no evidence that Tiddalik behaves in a thoughtful or friendly way. **C** is incorrect. Tiddalik's actions can be described as mean, but while Tiddalik may look ugly when filled up with water, there is no evidence that Tiddalik is an ugly frog.

2 This is a **judgement** question. **B** is correct. You read *They would have to get the water back somehow (see lines 5–6)*. You judge that the other animals realise that without water they would die. **A** is incorrect. The other animals are more worried about getting water for themselves than helping Tiddalik move. **C** is incorrect. It is true that they didn't have a plan at this stage, but the emergency was the fact that there was no water left.

3 This is a **judgement** question. **B** is correct. You judge that Tiddalik doesn't think the dances are funny. He does laugh at the eel's wild movements so you know he finds other things funny. **A** is incorrect because Tiddalik can see the eel's movements so his eyes can't be shut. **C** is incorrect because there is no evidence that the reason he doesn't laugh is to keep in the water he drank.

4 This is a **judgement** question. **C** is correct. The eel can't hold back its anger when the animals fail to make Tiddalik laugh. You judge that it does not realise its wild, angry body movements will make Tiddlik laugh and solve the animals' problem. **A** is incorrect. You judge that the eel moves its body in a wild way because it is so angry, not because it thinks it knows better than the others how to make Tiddalik laugh. **B** is incorrect. There is no evidence about how angry the eel felt at other times.

5 This is a **judgement** question. **B** is correct. You read *He shrank to his present size (see lines 9–10)* and that he *crept away (see line 11)*. You judge that the reason he would creep away to hide is that he feels bad—embarrassed and ashamed of himself. He doesn't want the other animals looking at him. **A** is incorrect. The other animals were very angry with him for being greedy. You judge that it is unlikely that Tiddalik would already look for more water. **C** is incorrect. It is true that frogs make their homes in reeds and mud but this is not the reason Tiddalik goes there. He goes there to hide from the animals.

6 This is a **judgement** question. You are likely to judge that the moral of this story is that it is important to share and not take everything for yourself.

Rikki-Tikki-Tavi (page 55)

1 C	2 A	3 B	4 B
5 B	6 See below		

Explanations

1 This is a **judgement** question. **C** is correct. You read the description of the mongoose and the fact that it had a *restless nose (see lines 4–5)*. You can visualise it poking its *restless nose* where it might not belong, sniffing out trouble, being nosy and getting into mischief. The narrator tells readers that the mongoose has a restless nose as a clue to its character. **A** is incorrect as there is no evidence that the mongoose sneezes at all. **B** is incorrect. The adjective *restless* does not tell you what the nose looked like. It describes how the character behaves.

2 This is a **judgement** question. **A** is correct. You read that the mongoose was swept along by the flood water *kicking and clucking (see line 9)*. The fact that it kicks shows you it fights the flood and tries to swim. The fact that it clucked tells you it complained about being

caught by the flood. You could judge that the mongoose might also cluck because it is angry and fighting the floodwater. **B** is incorrect as there is no evidence that the mongoose is always angry. **C** is incorrect because you cannot judge that the mongoose is a good swimmer just because it kicked.

3 This is a **judgement** question. **B** is correct. You read that the mongoose was caught in flood water and looked *very draggled indeed (see lines 11–12)*. You can judge that it looked wet and battered. (Note that *draggled* is a shortened form of the word 'bedraggled'.) **A** is incorrect. The sun is described as hot rather than the mongoose. **C** is incorrect. The mongoose is described as having a bottle-brush tail before it got caught in the flood.

4 This is a **judgement** question. **B** is correct. You should judge that a creature's head and habits are more important than its fur and tail in defining what sort of creature it is. You read that the mongoose's head looked like a weasel and its habits were like a weasel's. **A** and **C** are incorrect. You read that its fur and tail were like a cat's (**A**) and that it could fluff up its tail like a bottle brush (**C**).

5 This is a **judgement** question. **B** is correct. You read that the mongoose nearly drowned so you can judge the flood to be dangerous for some creatures. **A** is incorrect because nearly drowning is not fun. **C** is incorrect. The way the narrator tells of a high summer flood makes it sound like a common or regular event.

6 This is a **judgement** question. You read that the small boy said, "*Here's a dead mongoose. Let's have a funeral*" *(see line 12)*. You can judge that the boy jumped to the conclusion that the mongoose was dead without making sure. Perhaps he was excited about the idea of a funeral because he had buried dead pets and had funerals for them. He doesn't seem sad or concerned about finding a dead animal. He seems to think that a funeral might be something interesting to do like a game to play.

The Postman (page 56)

1 See below	2 C	3 A
4 A	5 See below	6 See below

Explanations

1 This is a **judgement** question. You judge that in 1921, when the poem was written, the posties were all men. They delivered letters on foot, took letters to the door and wore a uniform with a cap. None of these things are true of today's posties. Today, posties can be male or female.

2 This is a **judgement** question. **C** is correct. The poet imagines himself as a postman politely saying hello to the gentlemen he meets as he goes about his duties. (Notice that he doesn't expect to meet any ladies, only gentlemen.) **A** is incorrect. The postman's behaviour is polite and well mannered but he doesn't imagine himself being stern. **B** is incorrect. The postman is neither bossy nor strict in his behaviour.

3 This is a **judgement** question. **A** is correct. You judge that the poet imagines he would wear his uniform with pride. He thinks of how *very nice and neat (see line 5)* it would look. **B** and **C** are incorrect because there is no evidence to suggest that he would feel embarrassed or uncomfortable in his uniform.

4 This is a **judgement** question. **A** is correct. You judge that the poem was written to amuse the reader. The poet is enjoying having fun imagining himself doing what he judges to be an important job. **B** is incorrect. The poem describes what the boy imagines a postman does but the purpose of this is to share the humour of what he imagines. **C** is incorrect. The poet thinks of ways to be a perfect postman but this is part of the humour rather than a lesson about how to do a job.

5 This is a **judgement** question. The question *Would you? (see line 9)* asks readers to think whether they would choose to be a postman if they knew they'd get sore feet. You judge that asking this is a way for the poet to connect with the reader.

6 This is a **judgement** question. Answers will vary. You may judge, for example, that the illustration adds to the humour of the poem because it is different from what the words of the poem tell the reader. Or you may judge that it does not suit the poem well because the postman imagines saying good morning to gentlemen, not ladies. The ladies don't look pleased to see him either!

Multiculturalism (page 57)

1 A	2 A	3 B
4 A	5 See below	6 See below

Explanations

1 This is a **judgement** question. **A** is correct. You can judge that Mr King encourages his students to share their ideas openly. He listens to them and replies in a way that makes them feel he is interested in what they have to say. **B** is incorrect. There is no evidence that Mr King is impatient. **C** is incorrect. Mr King does not seem strict.

2 This is a **judgement** question. **A** is correct. Christos has a strong interest in multicultural food and his attitude in the discussion is enthusiastic. **B** is incorrect. There is no evidence that Christos is being unhelpful or annoying. **C** is incorrect because Christos joins in and shows interest in the discussion. There are no signs that he is bored.

3 This is a **judgement** question. **B** is correct. You judge that Adriana finds the idea of cultures mixing together interesting. She is keen to talk about her experience of the multicultural football round. She shares with the class that her father was born in Italy. **A** is incorrect. Adriana helps explain what multiculturalism means in a way that shows she is not confused about it. **C** is incorrect. Adriana does not show any sign of being worried.

4 This is a **judgement** question. **A** is correct. Adriana's survey is the best solution. This is because a survey means asking people questions. This might give the students the information they need. **B** is incorrect. May Britt's idea of a graph could also work well but you would first have to collect the information to put in the graph. **C** is incorrect. Christos's idea would not help very much. This is because a list of people's favourite foods may not tell you anything about their cultural background.

5 This is a **judgement** question. Answers will vary. There is no right or wrong answer. Your answer will depend on your own experiences. You might think that Mr King is the kind of teacher you'd like. You might think the children in the class seem very friendly. Remember to give reasons for your answer.

6 This is a **judgement** question. You are likely to judge that it does seem to be a good thing. The class is positive about multiculturalism. The children talk about different events organised to celebrate multiculturalism, such as the football round and the food festival. Adriana and May Britt enjoyed attending these events. The children also like the idea of tasting foods from different cultures, such as souvlaki and Swedish meatballs.

Mixed questions

My family (page 58)

1 C	2 B	3 A
4 A, B and C	5 C	6 See below

Explanations

1 This is a **fact-finding** question. **C** is correct. You read *They live with their dog, Bi Bi (see line 3)*. **A** is incorrect. Poodle is the breed of dog. **B** is incorrect. Gong Gong is a name Emily uses for her grandfather.

2 This is a **fact-finding** question. **B** is correct. You read *Every July Por Por and Gong Gong go back to Hong Kong (see line 8)*. **A** is incorrect because it doesn't tell when the grandparents visit Hong Kong. **C** is incorrect. It tells what the grandparents do in Hong Kong.

3 This is a **synthesis** question. **A** is correct. Paragraph one introduces the grandparents and their dog. Paragraph two tells what happens to the dog when the grandparents travel. **B** is incorrect as the text only discusses the grandparents because it tells about their dog. **C** is incorrect as walking the dog is mentioned only once at the end of the text.

4 This is an **inferring** question. **A, B** and **C** are correct. You read *I have to … take her for walks. She is not very well trained (see lines 10–11)*. You can work out that the dog might misbehave, chase birds and drag on the leash, because it is *not … well trained (see line 11)*.

5 This is a **language** question. **C** is correct. You read *Por Por says she doesn't mind (see line 11)*. You can work out that the word for grandmother is Por Por. You read *Bi Bi means baby in Cantonese (see lines 3–4)*. So you can work out that the word for grandfather must be Gong Gong. **A** and **B** are therefore incorrect.

6 This is a **judgement** question. You can judge that Bi Bi is treated like a baby. You might judge that the grandparents spoil her. Perhaps the grandparents didn't have the energy to train her when she was a puppy. Or the grandparents didn't know how to train her. Or the grandparents didn't want to try to train her. You read *She is not very well trained. Por Por says she doesn't mind (see lines 10–11)*. You can judge that the grandparents love Bi Bi just the way she is.

A visit from Mrs Snake (page 59)

1 B	2 Mrs Koala	3 B
4 A	5 See below	6 See below

Explanations

1 This is a **fact-finding** question. **B** is correct. You read that Mrs Koala *saw Mrs Snake slowly wriggling her way upwards (see lines 3–4)*. **A** is incorrect because Baby Koala is in Mrs Koala's pouch and she is not looking at him when she looks down the tree. **C** is incorrect because Mrs Magpie is not there.

2 This is a **fact-finding** question. You read the words *"Go away, Mrs Snake!" she [Mrs Koala] called in a loud voice (see line 5)*. In the illustration you can see that Mrs Koala is speaking to Mrs Snake.

3 This is a **synthesis** question. **B** is correct. The text is mainly about the threat to Baby Koala, or the danger he is in, from Mrs Snake. **A** is incorrect. No-one escapes in this text. **C** is incorrect. Mrs Snake says she will take Baby Koala for a ride but this doesn't happen.

4 This is an **inferring** question. **A** is correct. Mrs Koala doesn't trust anything Mrs Snake says. She thinks Mrs Snake is trying to trick her into letting her take Baby Koala away. **B** is incorrect. Mrs Koala thinks Mrs Snake lies to get what she wants and is not to be trusted. **C** is incorrect. Mrs Koala is frightened of Mrs Snake and does not believe that Mrs Snake wants to help her with Baby Koala.

5 This is a **language** question. The word *slyly* means 'in a sneaky or cunning way'. The 's' sounds in *said Mrs Snake slyly (see line 13)* imitate the sound of a snake hissing. The writer is letting readers know that Mrs Snake is being tricky and cunning with what she says. What Mrs Snake says is not to be trusted.

6 This is a **judgement** question. You could judge that Mrs Magpie would not send Mrs Snake. Mrs Snake is likely to be lying when she says this. She wants to hide the fact that she came to see Baby for her own reasons. You could also judge that Mrs Magpie may have sent Mrs Snake. Mrs Magpie might have wanted to get the snake away from her own babies or for some other reason.

My broken arm (page 60)

1 B	2 B	3 2, 1, 4, 3	4 C
5 C	6 See below		

Explanations

1 This is a **fact-finding** question. **B** is correct. You read *The doctor said I had a hairline fracture. That's a really thin crack in the bone (see lines 10–11)*. **A** is incorrect. A hairline fracture can happen to a bone anywhere in the body. A fracture is not a bone. **C** is incorrect. The hospital took an X-ray of the arm to see the hairline fracture.

2 This is a **fact-finding** question. **B** is correct. You read *Dad took me home and put an icepack on it. He said that would reduce the swelling (see lines 5–6)*. (Note that *reduce* means 'make lower or less'.) **A** and **C** are incorrect. The ice will not fix the arm or make it better.

3 This is a **synthesis** question. The sequence is 2, 1, 4, 3. 1 I went to the park. 2 I fell off the monkey bars. 3 I broke my arm. 4 I had an X-ray.

4 This is an **inferring** question. **C** is correct. Look at the photo. You can tell by the expression on the child's face that she is disappointed. **A** and **B** are incorrect. The child does not look excited or happy.

5 This is a **language** question. **C** is correct. Monkeys climb and swing by their arms. This is what children do on monkey bars. They climb and swing like monkeys. **A** is incorrect.

Monkeys don't climb on the bars in the playground. **B** is incorrect. The equipment is not called monkey bars because children use it to pretend to be monkeys.

6 This is a **judgement** question. You should judge that the monkey bars cannot be stupid. The writer's broken arm was an accident. It wasn't anyone's fault and it was not the fault of the monkey bars. Put yourself in the writer's position to understand how she feels. You can judge that she is annoyed because her arm is broken and she wants to be able to blame someone or something. This is why she calls the monkey bars *Stupid* (see line 13).

Roosters (page 61)

1 C	**2** B	**3** B	**4** A
5 A	**6** See below		

Explanations

1 This is a **fact-finding** question. **C** is correct. You read *The red combs on the roosters' heads are usually larger than the hens' combs* (see lines 4–5). **A** and **B** are incorrect because the roosters' combs are larger rather than smaller or the same size as hens' combs.

2 This is a **fact-finding** question. **B** is correct. You read *Roosters begin crowing at the crack of dawn* (see line 7). **A** and **C** are incorrect because roosters do not begin to crow at these times.

3 This is a **synthesis** question. **B** is correct. The only place where roosters' feathers are compared with hens' feathers is in paragraph one. **A** and **C** are incorrect. Paragraph two is about roosters crowing and looking after their flocks.

4 This is an **inferring** question. **A** is correct. A rooster's family is made up of his flock of female hens. **B** is incorrect because each rooster has a number of hens in his flock. **C** is incorrect because there are no crows included in a rooster's family.

5 This is a **language** question. **A** is correct. The phrase *crack of dawn* (see line 7) refers to very early in the morning. It is the time when the sun first begins to light the sky. You can work out that **B** is incorrect because you know the sky doesn't crack open. **C** is incorrect because if the sun has been up for a few hours, it must be after dawn.

6 This is a **judgement** question. Roosters keep a look out for their flock and warn them if danger is nearby.

Eddie's question (page 62)

1 C	**2** B	**3** B	**4** B
5 B	**6** See below		

Explanations

1 This is a **fact-finding** question. **C** is correct. You read *Mario's dad is taking Mario to see his sister play the drums* (see lines 2–3). This means that Mario's sister plays the drums. **A** is incorrect as Eddie is the writer. **B** is incorrect as you read that Mario's sister, rather than Mario, is playing drums.

2 This is a **fact-finding** question. **B** is correct. You read *It finishes at 9 pm* (see line 5). *It* refers to the concert. **A** is incorrect. This is when Mario's dad will collect Eddie. **C** is incorrect. This is the time that Mario's dad will bring Eddie home.

3 This is a **synthesis** question. **B** is correct. The reason for the invitation is that Mario's sister is playing in the concert. **A** is incorrect. This is what Eddie's mum can do to check on Eddie's information. **C** is incorrect as this is something Eddie might do if he goes to the concert.

4 This is an **inferring** question. **B** is correct. You can infer that the main reason for the Thai dinner is that it is Mario's sister's favourite food. She is playing in the concert. Her dad is proud of her so as a special treat the family will eat her choice for dinner. **A** is incorrect. There is no evidence in the text to confirm that there's nowhere else to eat. **C** might be true. Mario might like Thai too but that's not the main reason for the Thai dinner.

5 This is a **language** question. **B** is correct. *He* refers to Mario's dad. You read *Mario's dad's invited me … He said … He's going to* (see lines 5–6). This makes **A** and **C** incorrect.

6 This is a **judgement** question. You can judge that Eddie will be allowed to go with Mario's family once his mother has heard all the information again and checked with Mario's dad. You can tell that Eddie is excited because he talks without pause and with enthusiasm. You can judge that his mother is used to Eddie and Mario getting together after school. You can judge that Eddie is very comfortable and familiar with Mario's family.

A bluebottle sting (page 63)

1 B	**2** B	**3** C	**4** A
5 B	**6** See below		

Explanations

1 This is a **fact-finding** question. **B** is correct. You read *He splashed it off with sea water* (see lines 10–11). **A** and **C** are incorrect because ice water and vinegar are not what you use to splash off a tentacle.

2 This is a **fact-finding** question. **B** is correct. You read *Its long tentacle was wrapped around my arm* (see lines 7–8). **A** and **C** are incorrect because Ella was not stung on her leg or on her foot.

3 This is a **synthesis** question. **C** is correct. You read that after Ella was stung by the bluebottle her dad washed the tentacle off with sea water. **A** is incorrect. The heat pack was used after the tentacle was washed off. **B** is incorrect. Ella did run out of the water but this did not treat her sting. The first thing Ella's dad did to treat the sting was get the tentacle off.

4 This is an **inferring** question. **A** is correct. You read *The pain was horrible. It lasted for ages but a heat pack helped a bit … the latest research says hot water or a heat pack works best* (see lines 13–15). **B** and **C** are incorrect. Neither ice nor sea water are suggested to help with pain.

5 This is a **language** question. **B** is correct. The *latest* is the newest or most recent. The word *research* refers to making a study of something. The prefix *re-* means 'again' and *search* means 'look carefully for something'. If you research a subject (e.g. bluebottle stings) you make a close study of it to find out more about it. **A** is incorrect. What many people think can be different from what *the latest research* tells us. Ella's dad is a lifesaver so he needs to keep up to date with the latest research into bluebottle stings. **C** is incorrect. Ella's dad is not giving his opinion. He is saying what *the latest research* has found out.

6 This is a **judgement** question. You judge that Ella's dad acted calmly when Ella came running to him yelling.

He tells Ella what she should not do and then patiently explains the reasons for what needs doing. He uses his expert knowledge to treat the sting.

Furry lifesaver (page 64)

1 B	**2** its mouth	**3** B	**4** B
5 C	**6** See below		

Explanations

1 This is a **fact-finding** question. **B** is correct. You read *a huge bear rescued a crow from drowning in its enclosure* (see lines 3–5). **A** is incorrect. The bear rescued the crow. It did not try to eat the crow. **C** is incorrect. The crow was wet and muddy after it was rescued from drowning.

2 This is a **fact-finding** question. You read in the text that the bear used its mouth to lift the crow out onto the dirt.

3 This is a **synthesis** question. **B** is correct. The whole text is about the bear saving the crow from drowning. **A** is incorrect because the text is not about the zoo although it is where the bear lives. **C** is incorrect. This is a fact in the text but the text is mainly about the bear's act of kindness, rather than the crow being wet and muddy.

4 This is an **inferring** question. **B** is correct. You can infer that the writer was not surprised that the bear helped the crow. You read *It's not surprising that the bear showed kindness towards the bird* (see line 14). **A** is incorrect. The crow is described as being surprised, not the writer. **C** is incorrect. Zoo visitors, rather than the writer, were *amazed* (see line 3).

5 This is a **language** question. **C** is correct. You read *The bear watched it for a moment. Then the bear lumbered over* (see lines 9–10). You need to visualise what the bear looked like as it moved across its enclosure. It moved heavily because it was huge. **A** is incorrect. You can work out that the huge bear did not rush quickly. It took its time, watching the crow for a moment, then it *lumbered over*. **B** is incorrect. You can work out that the bear did not need to walk carefully in its own enclosure.

6 This is a **judgement** question. You might make any of the following judgements.
- It was a captive bear, not a wild bear.
- It had no need to kill for food.
- I was not interested in killing for sport.
- It felt sorry for the crow.
- It was smart enough to work out that the crow was in trouble and it knew how to save it.

The Great Mango Mystery (page 65)

1 Prince Jason	**2** A	**3** B	**4** A
5 C	**6** See below		

Explanations

1 This is a **fact-finding** question. You read *Prince Jason was hailed as a hero* (see line 17). He was a hero because he solved the mystery.

2 This is a **fact-finding** question. **A** is correct. You read *all the mangoes had disappeared. Phhht. Gone! This made the people of the kingdom cross and grumpy* (see lines 2–4). The word *This* helps you connect the people being cross and grumpy to the reason: that all the mangoes had disappeared. **B** is incorrect because the people hadn't asked Prince Jason to look for the mangoes at this point in the story. **C** is incorrect as there is no evidence in the text that the people were hungry.

3 This is a **synthesis** question. **B** is correct. Queen Snow and King Akmal create a problem for the people of Desa Kiara because they don't share the mangoes with them. Once they promise to share the mangoes, all is well. **A** is incorrect. The story is not about greed. **C** is incorrect. The story is not about telling lies.

4 This is an **inferring** question. **A** is correct. The parents trembled when their son used *his steeliest voice* (see line 13). He caused them to tremble in fear because they were guilty. **B** is incorrect. There is no evidence in the text that Prince Jason's parents had grown old and shaky. **C** is incorrect. Prince Jason's parents immediately confessed and promised not to repeat their crime. This shows that their trembling comes from fear of their son's anger, rather than from their own anger or rage.

5 This is a **language** question. **C** is correct. You read *He practised his sternest face in front of the mirror. Now he was ready to confront his parents* (see lines 11–12). The Prince had realised that his parents had stolen the mangoes. He went to meet them face to face and challenge them about their crime. **A** is incorrect because Prince Jason did not move to the front. **B** is incorrect because there is no evidence that Prince Jason is unkind.

6 This is a **judgement** question. You are likely to judge that Prince Jason behaves like a hero in this story because he is wise and brave.
- He listened to the troubles of his people.
- He confronted his parents about their crime.
- He solved the mystery.
- He made the people of the kingdom happy.

Stay away! (page 66)

1 a magpie	**2** B	**3** A	**4** B
5 C	**6** See below		

Explanations

1 This is a **fact-finding** question. You read that Maggie *looked at her three newly hatched magpie chicks* (see lines 13–14).

2 This is a **fact-finding** question. **B** is correct. You read that *Maggie and Marty sat on a branch guarding their nest in the tree above the kindergarten* (see lines 2–3). **A** is incorrect. They do not live at the kindergarten. **C** is incorrect. They do not live in a nest.

3 This is a **synthesis** question. **A** is correct. Marty swoops because he is defending his nest during nesting season. **B** and **C** are incorrect. Marty only hates cyclists and defends his territory from them during nesting season and not all the time.

4 This is an **inferring** question. **B** is correct. The text gives Maggie's point of view but both magpies think the cyclist should *stay away*. **A** is incorrect. You know the cyclist would want the magpie to stay away but the cyclist's point of view is not given in the text. **C** is incorrect. The evidence in the text tells you that kindy children like the magpies.

5 This is a **language** question. **C** is correct. You read *They'd need her and Marty to protect them for a few weeks yet. They were so defenceless* (see lines 14–16). The suffix *-less*

means 'without'. You can work out that *defenceless* means 'without defence'. The magpie chicks could not look after themselves. They were open to danger. **A** and **B** are incorrect. This is what the magpie parents do. The parents protect their young and resist attack from cyclists. This is not what *defenceless* means.

6 This is a **judgement** question. Think about what Marty does and why he behaves like this. You should judge that Marty is only defending his chicks. This is Marty's natural behavior. You would be incorrect if you judged Marty to be cruel or mean to the cyclist.

What is a cloud? (page 67)

1 millions	**2** A	**3** A
4 A	**5** See below	**6** See below

Explanations

1 This is a **fact-finding** question. You read *A cloud is … Millions of water droplets / tossing in the air* (see lines 7–8).

2 This is a **fact-finding** question. **A** is correct. You read *A cloud is …. A stormy black frown that scowls* (see lines 2–11). **B** and **C** are incorrect as the storm clouds in this poem are not described as grey or white.

3 This is a **synthesis** question. **A** is correct. Sometimes the poet thinks about looking down at clouds. At other times she is beneath the clouds looking up. **B** is incorrect because the poet describes clouds she has seen or imagined from different positions or places. **C** is incorrect. There is no evidence that the poet is ever inside them.

4 This is an **inferring** question. **A** is correct. People turn up their faces to see if rain is beginning to fall from the *stormy black* (see line 11) clouds. **B** is incorrect. It is people's faces that are upturned, not their noses. **C** is incorrect. The poet does not suggest that people hope it won't rain.

5 This is a **language** question. The word *lonely* (see line 13) suggests to readers that the cloud, like a person, has feelings. It feels sad because there are no other clouds nearby. It drifts about alone in the immense sky looking for a friend. A sad, wistful mood is created.

6 This is a **judgement** question. You are likely to judge that the poet is fascinated by clouds. She expresses a sense of wonder at the magical way they take over her thoughts; how they change themselves from droplets of water into amazing shapes and forms; and how they create different moods and feelings.

CONCERT to SAVE THIS POSSUM (page 68)

1 See below	**2** B	**3** A	**4** B
5 B	**6** See below		

Explanations

1 This is a **fact-finding** question. You read that these possums *only live in three very tiny areas in the high mountains of NSW and Victoria* (see lines 5–6).

2 This is a **fact-finding** question. **B** is correct. You read *All money raised will go towards captive breeding programs so the Mountain pygmy-possum doesn't become extinct* (see lines 14–15). **A** and **C** are therefore incorrect.

3 This is a **synthesis** question. **A** is correct. Connect ideas from across the text to work out that the poster is advertising a concert. **B** is incorrect. The concert ticket sales will go towards helping the possum but ways to help the possum are not listed on the poster. **C** is incorrect. The poster does inform people about the possums and their problems but this is not the main purpose of the poster.

4 This is an **inferring** question. **B** is correct. You can infer that, because climate change is making the mountains warmer, foxes and cats will move in and they will kill and eat the possums. **A** is incorrect. Bogong moths are eaten by possums. The moths don't eat possums. **C** is incorrect. Hunters don't kill the possums.

5 This is a **language** question. **B** is correct. *THIS POSSUM* (see line 1) refers to the species of Mountain pygmy-possum and not just the possum in the drawing (**A**) or any other kind of pygmy-possum (**C**).

6 This is a **judgement** question. You need to decide whether or not this poster would encourage people to go to the concert so that a lot of money is raised to help the possums. You might judge that the poster does a good job because:
- it shows a picture of the possum and its size compared to a person's finger
- it tells the time and date of the concert and what entertainment the concert includes
- it tells some facts about problems the possum has in the wild
- it tells people what the money will be for.

You might judge that the poster will not be successful. You might think that the poster does not make the concert seem interesting enough to make people want to attend.

Animal sounds (page 69)

1 B	**2** A, B and C	**3** B
4 A	**5** B	**6** See below

Explanations

1 This is a **fact-finding** question. **B** is correct. You read *bats … make sounds to find each other in the dark* (see lines 9–10). **A** and **C** are incorrect because snails and roosters do not use sound to find each other in the dark.

2 This is a **fact-finding** question. **A**, **B** and **C** are correct. You read *Cockatoos … also copy human speech. Parrots and budgerigars copy human speech too* (see lines 12–14).

3 This is a **synthesis** question. **B** is correct. The main idea in the text is that animals use sound to communicate with each other and with humans. **A** is incorrect. Animals can communicate with people but it is not true that animals talk in the same way as humans. **C** is incorrect. It is true that animals make sounds but this is not the main idea in the text.

4 This is an **inferring** question. **A** is correct. You read *Different species of animal make different sounds* (see line 11). You can work out from this that a single species will make similar, rather than different, sounds. The sounds they make are part of what makes them a species. **B** is incorrect because different species make different sounds from each other, but a single species makes similar sounds. **C** is incorrect. Most species make sounds.

5 This is a **language** question. **B** is correct. The word bells is the odd one out. It is not a word for a sound (onomatopoeia). **A** and **C** are incorrect. The words squeak and croak are words for sounds made by animals.

6 This is a **judgement** question. Answers will vary. You might decide, for example, that a bird that can copy human speech is the cleverest.

Bones of giant animal found (page 70)

1 B	2 C	3 A	4 C
5 C	6 See below		

Explanations

1 This is a **fact-finding** question. **B** is correct. You read *The bones were dug up in far northern Queensland (see lines 5–7)*. **A** is incorrect because they were dug up in the north, not the south, of Queensland. **C** is true and partly correct but the answer 'far northern Queensland' is more exact.

2 This is a **fact-finding** question. **C** is correct. You read *Scientists believe that diprotodons looked like giant wombats (see lines 17–19)*. **A** is incorrect as the diprotodons did not look like giants, although they were giant-sized animals. **B** is incorrect. Diprotodons did not look like small cars, although they were a similar size.

3 This is a **synthesis** question. **A** is correct. The main purpose of this newspaper article is to report the discovery of the bones of a giant-sized animal. **B** is incorrect. The article does describe diprotodons but this is not its main purpose. **C** is incorrect. The article does not tell a story about diprotodons.

4 This is an **inferring** question. **C** is correct. You read *'We are pleased because we found the skull and jaws and most of the rest of the skeleton. It is rare to find whole diprotodon skeletons,' (see lines 8–13)*. This suggests the team found most of the skeleton. **A** and **B** are incorrect. You can work out they were unable to find all of the skeleton (**A**) and that they found more than a small number of bones (**B**).

5 This is a **language** question. **C** is correct. The word *giant (see line 19)* is used to describe the unusually large bones that were found. **A** and **B** are incorrect. The word *giant* is an adjective describing the size of the bones. Use of the word giant does not suggest that the bones are not real bones or that the report is a fairytale.

6 This is a **judgement** question. You read about other bones of giant-sized animals being discovered nearby. You judge that scientists will want to look for more skeletons in the area. This is because new discoveries are likely to provide scientists with information about the animals and what caused them to become extinct.

Tonsillectomy (page 71)

1 A	2 B	3 C	4 C
5 B	6 See below		

Explanations

1 This is a **fact-finding** question. **A** is correct. You read *Put your mother on the phone for me, please. A grandfather's job is to make sure you have many ice-creams (see lines 14–15)*. **B** and **C** are therefore incorrect.

2 This is a **fact-finding** question. **B** is correct. You read *I keep getting infections and missing school (see line 6)*. **A** is incorrect. Large tonsils can get in the way of breathing but they do not choke you. **C** is incorrect. The child in the text says his tonsils are really big but this alone is not a reason to have them taken out.

3 This is a **synthesis** question. **C** is correct. At the beginning of the text the grandfather says *Bonjour* and Jean Pierre says *Hello (see lines 2–3)*. At the end of the text Pépère tells the child to put his mother on the phone. Think about what would happen next in the conversation. Pépère would say Bonjour (Hello) to Jean Pierre's mother. **A** is incorrect. This information was stated earlier in the text. **B** is incorrect. This is something the doctor in the photo might have said before the conversation of the text.

4 This is an **inferring** question. **C** is correct. Read between the lines to work out that Pépère and his grandson have a close and loving relationship. The grandchild shares his news with Pépère. Pépère is interested to hear his news and speaks kindly to him. **A** is incorrect. You can infer that English is Pépère's second language but there is nothing in the text to say that this makes the relationship difficult. **B** is incorrect. The evidence in the text shows that the relationship is not awkward, even though they might live far apart.

5 This is a **language** question. **B** is correct. The title of the text is *Tonsillectomy*. The boy tells his grandfather about having to get his tonsils out. You should work out that a tonsillectomy is an operation to remove tonsils. **A** and **C** are therefore incorrect.

6 This is a **judgement** question. You can judge that Pépère is confident that his grandson will be fine. He might think his grandson is a little worried so he reassures him by being light-hearted and focusing only on a holiday in hospital and eating ice-cream.

Wipe-out! (page 72)

1 C	2 A	3 A	4 C
5 A	6 See below		

Explanations

1 This is a **fact-finding** question. **C** is correct. You read *Wipe-out! The new soap-in-a-bottle (see lines 2–3)*. **A** is incorrect. Wipe-out! includes germ-fighting ingredients but this is not what Wipe-out! is. **B** is incorrect. Children can get a free sticker if they buy Wipe-out! but Wipe-out! is not a free sticker.

2 This is a **fact-finding** question. **A** is correct. You read *for just a few cents a day (see lines 10–11)*. **B** and **C** are incorrect. These amounts are incorrect guesses at what Wipe-out! might cost over a longer time period than that given in the text.

3 This is a **synthesis** question. **A** is correct. The text is an advertisement. Its purpose is to convince people to buy soap. You read *Wipe-out! The new soap-in-a-bottle ... Buy now (see lines 2–7)*. **B** is incorrect. The purpose of the text is to sell soap, not to get people to kill germs. **C** is incorrect. The text does not tell people to collect the stickers. You read *Children will love the ... stickers (see lines 27–29)*.

4 This is an **inferring** question. **C** is correct. You read *Wipe-out! The new soap-in-a-bottle. Wipes out germs with powerful germ-fighting ingredients (see lines 2–6)*.

Wipe-out! uses powerful ingredients to kill germs. **A** is incorrect. This is what Wipe-out! is, not what it does. **B** is incorrect. Light-up! gel and UV light are used to show people the germs on their hands. This is not what Wipe-out! does.

5 This is a **language** question. **A** is correct. To wipe out something is to destroy it completely. This makes the name Wipe-out! sound active and powerful. The exclamation mark as part of the name emphasises this. It sounds as if germs have no hope of surviving when Wipe-out! is used on them. **B** is incorrect. The advertisement connects using Wipe-out! with staying healthy and germ-free but the name is not itself linked with ideas about staying healthy. **C** is incorrect. The name Wipe-out! doesn't sound expensive. A name like 'Liquid Gold' would sound expensive but not Wipe-out!

6 This is a **judgement** question. Answers will vary. You might like the idea of seeing Wipe-out! in action. You might want to use the Light-up! germ gel and UV light to see the germs and then see if Wipe-out! really does make them disappear. You might judge that Wipe-out! sounds fun to use. You might want to collect the free stickers. Or you might state that Wipe-out! doesn't interest you. You might not care about a soap product or free stickers.

The herd (page 73)

1 C	**2** herd	**3** C
4 C	**5** A	**6** See below

Explanations

1 This is a **fact-finding** question. **C** is correct. You read *Savannah was the herd's leader, the matriarch* (see line 2). The text is about her and her attitude and leadership. Each of the three paragraphs starts with *Savannah*. **A** is incorrect. Lox is the male elephant that is being told to leave the herd. **B** is incorrect. Chad is Lox's older brother. Chad is mentioned only once.

2 This is a **fact-finding** question. A word for a group of elephants is *herd*. You read *Savannah was the herd's leader* (see line 2).

3 This is a **synthesis** question. **C** is correct. You read *Savannah gave him a gentle nudge with her trunk. He needed to be on his way* (see line 6). You can work out that Lox will leave the herd. He has to. *That was the way of the bulls* (see lines 7–8). **A** is incorrect. Savannah nudges Lox gently. The terms *nudged* and *coaxing* (see line 10) are gentle movements. You can work out that Savannah will not get angry with Lox. **B** is incorrect. You read *Savannah nudged him again, coaxing him away from the herd* (see line 10). You can work out that Lox will not be allowed to stay with the herd any longer.

4 This is an **inferring** question. **C** is correct. Read between the lines to work out that the female elephants and younger elephants live together in a herd. As soon as they are old enough, male elephants move away from the herd. **A** is incorrect. You read *The herd sometimes saw Lox's older brother … and his cousins at the waterhole* (see lines 8–9). This does not suggest that they live at the waterhole. They just visit the waterhole for a drink and then they roam away. **B** is incorrect. You read *He could live with other young bulls, if he wanted to, or roam on his own* (see lines 6–7). You can work out that younger males have a choice. Not all will prefer to roam on their own.

5 This is a **language** question. **A** is correct. You read *Savannah was the herd's leader, the matriarch. All eyes turned towards her* (see line 2). You can work out that the leader or matriarch of the elephant herd is a female elephant called Savannah. *Matriarch* is used to refer to a female head of any family, not just elephants. **B** is incorrect because a king is a male and Savannah is a female. **C** is incorrect because a matriarch is the powerful female and not just any mature (grown-up) elephant.

6 This is a **judgement** question. Savannah was not worried about Lox. The male elephants or bulls leave the herd when they are teenagers and so Savannah wanted Lox to leave. She nudged him with her trunk to push him out. She knew he could live with the other young bulls if he did not want to roam alone yet. You can judge that she was not worried about him leaving the herd.

Sandy's Animal Shelter (page 74)

1 B	**2** C	**3** C	**4** B
5 B	**6** See below		

Explanations

1 This is a **fact-finding** question. **B** is correct. Staff at the shelter clean kennels and wash dishes. You read the fact in the text: *Some days we don't even have time to pat the animals. We just clean kennels and wash dishes* (see lines 4–6). **A** is incorrect. The statement applies to older animals and not staff. You read *Those older animals get so confused. They don't know why they are at the shelter. They did have families once* (see lines 16–17). **C** is incorrect. You can read that staff have too much work to do to play with animals all day.

2 This is a **fact-finding** question. **C** is correct. You read *People choose puppies and kittens rather than older animals* (see lines 13–14). **A** and **B** are not facts in the text and are therefore incorrect.

3 This is a **synthesis** question. **C** is correct. The text is about staff and volunteers, as well as animals, at an animal shelter. **A** and **B** are incorrect. They are each only part of the answer because they don't include the people working at the shelter.

4 This is an **inferring** question. **B** is correct. Animals at the shelter need blankets because it is the beginning of winter. **A** and **C** are correct. Staff might feel the cold but the blanket donations are needed for the animals at the shelter.

5 This is a **language** question. **B** is correct. The text uses *neglect* (see line 9) to mean ignore. The writer worries that volunteers spend more time with the dogs at the shelter than the cats. The writer tells volunteers not to ignore (forget about) the cats. You read *They* [cats] *need attention too* (see lines 9–10). **A** and **C** are incorrect. Animals at the shelter may have been lost or hurt in the past but this is not what the writer means by *neglect* in the text.

6 This is a **judgement** question. The workers are the staff and volunteers. You read *we don't even have time to pat the animals* (see line 5) and *It's difficult to rehome older animals … That's heartbreaking* (see lines 13–14). You also read *older animals get so confused* (see line 16). You can judge that workers at the shelter worry about the happiness of the animals and finding new homes for them. You can judge that workers care about the animals and would like to be able to do more for them.

Grandpa's school report (page 75)

1 Jim Brown	**2** C	**3** A
4 B	**5** C	**6** See below

Explanations

1. This is a **fact-finding** question. You read *Yearly Report* [for] *Jim Brown (see lines 3–4)*.
2. This is a **fact-finding** question. **C** is correct. You read *Art … He* [Jim] *works very hard (see line 10)*. **A** and **B** are incorrect as the comments do not say that Jim worked very hard in these subjects.
3. This is a **synthesis** question. **A** is correct. Jim's community work is something he does outside of studying school subjects. It belongs in the *General comment (see lines 11–12)* space. **B** and **C** are incorrect. Maths and Science are school subjects and are not to do with community work.
4. This is an **inferring** question. **B** is correct. The only subject Jim works hard at, and gets excellent results in, is Art. You can work out that this makes it likely that Art is his favourite subject. **A** and **C** are incorrect. Jim doesn't try hard and spends time dreaming during these subjects so these are not likely to be his favourite subjects.
5. This is a **language** question. **C** is correct. The word *must* in this sentence is very definite. It is a strong statement. It is an order from the Form Master. **A** is incorrect. The words *could probably* in this sentence suggest it is possible but not definite. **B** is incorrect. The word *should* in this sentence means it is something he should do, but it is not certain that he will do it.
6. This is a **judgement** question. You should judge that the Form Master does not seem to like him very much. He only has one nice comment to make about him (Art). You might also guess that Jim causes problems when he brings animals to school.

Rufus (page 76)

1 Jasmine	**2** B	**3** B, A, C	**4** B
5 A	**6** C		

Explanations

1. This is a **fact-finding** question. You read the label on the photo—*Jasmine and Rufus (see line 12)*—and you read *This is me with my dog, Rufus (see line 2)*. You know that Jasmine has written the text about her dog.
2. This is a **fact-finding** question. **B** is correct. You read *His owners had moved from a house to a home unit and couldn't take Rufus with them (see lines 3–4)*. **A** is incorrect. Rufus's old owners may have wanted to find him a good home but there is no evidence in the text to confirm this. **C** is incorrect. You can't tell from the text that Rufus's old owners didn't want him. They might have kept him if they had not moved into a unit.
3. This is a **synthesis** question. The sequence is First: **B** Rufus was left at the animal shelter. Second: **A** Jasmine found Rufus at the animal shelter. Third: **C** Rufus went to live with Jasmine.
4. This is an **inferring** question. **B** is correct. You read *Rufus means red (see line 2)*. You should work out that Rufus was named by his first owners because he has reddish fur. When these owners left Rufus at the animal shelter they would have given his name and other details. **A** and **C** are incorrect. Rufus would not have needed to be named by shelter staff or by Jasmine.
5. This is a **language** question. **A** is correct. You read *Rufus was already an old dog when we got him. He was twelve. Dad said he was no spring chicken (see lines 5–6)*. *Spring chicken* is a saying that means something is young. Rufus was *no spring chicken* because he was already twelve years old. You may know this is old in dog years. **B** is incorrect as Rufus is an old dog. **C** is incorrect. The saying is not used to tell people that Rufus is a dog and not a chicken.
6. This is a **judgement** question. **C** is correct. You read *Sometimes I wonder whether Rufus misses his old family. (see lines 9–10)*. Jasmine puts herself in Rufus's position and thinks how sad she would feel if her family left her behind. **A** is incorrect. Jasmine cannot really know that Rufus feels abandoned. **B** is incorrect. Jasmine is not sad that Rufus is old. She just feels sad when she imagines what Rufus might think about his old family.

My friend from Iraq (page 77)

1 Iraq, Australia, Afghanistan, Somalia, Sri Lanka				
2 C	**3** C	**4** A	**5** B	**6** B

Explanations

1. This is a **fact-finding** question. You read *They have come to Australia from faraway places like Iraq, Afghanistan, Somalia and Sri Lanka (see lines 12–13)*.
2. This is a **fact-finding** question. **C** is correct. You read *My friend Hariq escaped from the war in Iraq … They were refugees (see lines 2–4)*. **A** is incorrect. The writer's dad is a volunteer. **B** is incorrect. Hariq is the writer's friend now but not when he first came to Australia.
3. This is a **synthesis** question. **C** is correct. The text is about the writer's friend, Hariq. Paragraph one introduces Hariq. Paragraph two describes Hariq's problems at school. Paragraph three tells how the writer's dad helps Hariq and other children. **A** is incorrect. The text is about Hariq but not Iraq. **B** is incorrect. The text is not about the writer's dad except how he helps at the Homework Centre.
4. This is an **inferring** question. **A** is correct. You read that Hariq found homework very difficult at first but now he is a star pupil at the Homework Centre. **B** is incorrect. Hariq still goes to school. The Homework Centre is for after school. **C** is incorrect. He has not become a refugee. He was a refugee when he first got to Australia.
5. This is a **language** question. **B** is correct. You read *My friend Hariq escaped from the war in Iraq. He came to Australia with his mother, his father and his sister. They were refugees (see lines 2–4)*. **A** is incorrect. Refugees can be adults as well as children. **C** is incorrect. Refugees also come from other places and not just Iraq.
6. This is a **judgement** question. **B** is correct. You can judge that the writer is proud of his dad and also that he or she is interested in Dad's work at the Centre. **A** is incorrect. The writer is not surprised about his or her dad's volunteer work. **C** is incorrect. The writer has made friends with Hariq and does not seem jealous.

The punishment (page 78)

1 the Greek gods	**2** B	**3** B
4 A	**5** A	**6** See below

Explanation

1 This is a **fact-finding** question. You read *He* [the king] *did things that made the Greek gods very angry* (see lines 3–4).

2 This is a **fact-finding** question. **B** is correct. You read *The god of the underworld came up to earth. He brought handcuffs with him to capture the king* (see lines 4–6). **A** and **C** are incorrect. There is no evidence in the text that the god used rope or poison.

3 This is a **synthesis** question. **B** is correct. The king tricked the god when the god tried to capture him (**B**). Then the king escaped (**C**) and after that the god punished the king (**A**). This makes **A** and **C** incorrect.

4 This is an **inferring** question. **A** is correct. You read *There was once a king who thought he was clever. He did things that made the Greek gods very angry* (see lines 2–4). You can work out that the king did these things because he was not afraid of the gods. **B** and **C** are incorrect because there is no evidence that the king admired or looked up to the gods.

5 This is a **language** question. **A** is correct. The phrase *all over again* (see line 14) means repeating the same thing over and over. **B** is incorrect. To do something over and over may not be to do it quickly. **C** is incorrect. To do something over and over and never finish the task is more times than often.

6 This is a **judgement** question. You judge that the god was angry with the king. He had tricked him and trapped him in his own handcuffs. The god made the punishment cruel to get his revenge on the king.

Animal dads (page 79)

1 fry	**2** a chick	**3** C
4 B	**5** See below	**6** See below

Explanations

1 This is a **fact-finding** question. You read *The eggs hatch inside his pouch. The tiny fry fend for themselves* (see lines 5–6).

2 This is a **fact-finding** question. You read *The egg hatches in two months. The mother penguin comes back to feed her chick* (see lines 13–15).

3 This is a **synthesis** question. **C** is correct. You read the title, *Animal dads* (see line 1). Both texts are about animal dads and how they care for their young. **A** is incorrect because it doesn't focus on the dads. **B** is incorrect because the text is not about all animals that lay eggs.

4 This is an **inferring** question. **B** is correct. You can work out that the ice would be too cold for the egg and the egg would crack. You should also know that birds sit on eggs to keep them warm in the nest until they hatch. The penguin needs to keep its egg warm. **A** is incorrect because water would not hurt an egg. **C** is incorrect. An egg could not make ice crack. An eggshell is more fragile than ice.

5 This is a **language** question. A pouch is like a pocket or a fold of skin. The pouch keeps the baby or babies safe until they can come out into the world.

6 This is a **judgement** question. You should judge that once the fry leave the dad's pouch they have to fend for themselves, so many will get eaten by predators. The seahorse needs to have hundreds of babies for a few to survive to adulthood. The Emperor penguin only has one baby because it takes two parents to share childcare duties in the icy-cold environment. The chick could not survive on its own and the parents could not manage to look after more than one chick at a time.

The song of the magic pudding (page 80)

1 a pot	**2** B	**3** C	**4** A
5 B	**6** B		

Explanations

1 This is a **fact-finding** question. You read "*O, who would be a puddin', / A puddin' in a pot,*' (see lines 2–3).

2 This is a **fact-finding** question. **B** is correct. You read *A puddin' which is stood on / A fire which is hot?*' (see lines 4–5).

3 This is a **synthesis** question. **C** is correct. The puddin' uses the song to complain about its miserable life. **A** is incorrect. The song is not a story. **B** is incorrect. The song includes information about the puddin's life but its purpose is to complain about that life.

4 This is an **inferring** question. **A** is correct. The poem is a complaint by the puddin' about its life. It gets put on a fire and eaten when it is cooked. No wonder it looks cross and sad in the picture! **B** is incorrect. It is true that the puddin' dislikes being in a pot (its hat in the picture) but this is only part of the reason. **C** is incorrect. There is no evidence that the puddin' wants to frighten the reader.

5 This is a **language** question. **B** is correct. The puddin' complains about being a puddin'. You read *O sad indeed* (see line 6). **A** is incorrect. The adjective *hot* (see line 12) is not used to describe how the puddin' feels. It is used by the puddin' to describe the fire and also when talking about the hot or burning stomach ache it hopes people get when they eat it. **C** is incorrect. You can tell that the puddin' is not happy.

6 This is a **judgement** question. **B** is correct. You read *I hope you get the stomach ache / For eatin' me a lot* (see lines 10–11). The puddin' hopes this because it wants to get its revenge and pay back those who eat it. **A** is incorrect. It is not simply because it is nasty and mean. The puddin' has a good reason for its unkind wishes. **C** is incorrect. The puddin' may be in a grumpy mood but this is not the reason it wants the people who eat it to get a stomach ache.

Dinosaurs (page 81)

1 C	**2** A	**3** B	**4** C
5 C	**6** See below		

Explanations

1 This is a **fact-finding** question. **C** is correct. You read *Dinosaurs lived on earth a very long time ago* (see line 2). **A** and **B** are incorrect because they are not facts in the text.

2 This is a **fact-finding** question. **A** is correct. You read *By the time humans lived on earth, dinosaurs had become extinct* (see lines 2–3). **B** and **C** are incorrect because dinosaurs lived on earth before humans, not after or at the same time as they did.

3 This is a **synthesis** question. **B** is correct. The whole text explains how we know about dinosaurs. Paragraph one introduces the topic of dinosaurs and asks *How … do we know anything about dinosaurs?* (see line 4). Paragraph 2 explains that fossils tell us about dinosaurs. Paragraph 3 explains what fossils tell us about dinosaurs. Paragraph 4 tells us that *Without fossils we'd know nothing at all about dinosaurs!* (see line 14). **A** is incorrect. The text does tell what fossils are but this information is only one part of paragraph 2. **C** is incorrect. The text does not explain how dinosaurs became extinct.

4 This is an **inferring** question. **C** is correct. You read *Fossils of dinosaur teeth tell what kinds of food different dinosaurs ate … plant eaters had blunt teeth* (see lines 11–12). Read between the lines to work out that dinosaurs with long, sharp teeth would have eaten meat. Sharp teeth can tear at flesh. Creatures alive today that have sharp teeth include sharks, lions and crocodiles. **A** and **B** are incorrect. You can infer that dinosaurs did not need long, sharp teeth to eat insects or plants.

5 This is a **language** question. **C** is correct. You read *Paleontology is the study of fossils* (see line 10). This suggests that paleontologists are people who study fossils. Suffixes *-er*, *-or* and *-ist* are used for people (e.g. garden—gardener; invention—inventor, dentistry—dentist). **A** is incorrect. Some of the fossils a paleontologist studies might not be from extinct plants or animals, just things that were alive a long time ago. **B** is incorrect because the fossils a paleontologist studies are not living things.

6 This is a **judgement** question. You might judge that being a paleontologist sounds interesting or exciting—digging up fossils, discovering fossils and examining fossils. Or you might judge it would be a boring job because you are more interested in the present than the past.

Marking grid for section 2: Mixed questions (pages 58–81)

Student name: ______________________

Use ✓ or ✗ to record correct and incorrect answers in the columns. Look for patterns of errors to identify areas that require revision.

Text title	Page	Date completed	1 Fact-finding	2 Synthesis	3 Inferring	4 Language	5 Judgement
My family	58						
A visit from Mrs Snake	59						
My broken arm	60						
Roosters	61						
Eddie's question	62						
A bluebottle sting	63						
Furry lifesaver	64						
The Great Mango Mystery	65						
Stay away!	66						
What is a cloud?	67						
CONCERT to SAVE THIS POSSUM	68						
Animal sounds	69						
Bones of giant animal found	70						
Tonsillectomy	71						
Wipe-out!	72						
The herd	73						
Sandy's Animal Shelter	74						
Grandpa's school report	75						
Rufus	76						
My friend from Iraq	77						
The punishment	78						
Animal dads	79						
The song of the magic pudding	80						
Dinosaurs	81						

Notes